Wishes come in Threes

Wishes come in Threes

ANDY JONES

WALKER BOOKS

First published 2022 by Walker Books Ltd
87 Vauxhall Walk, London SE11 5HJ

2 4 6 8 10 9 7 5 3 1

Text © 2022 Andy Jones
Cover illustration by Magarida Esteves

This book has been typeset in Active, Berkeley Oldstyle and Impress

Printed and bound by CPI Group (UK) Ltd, Croydon CR0 4YY

British Library Cataloguing in Publication Data:
a catalogue record for this book is available from the British Library

ISBN 978-1-5295-0088-2

www.walker.co.uk

MIX
Paper from
responsible sources
FSC® C171272

To Evie and Ruby

This story was inspired by you

x

Fort #57

One thing I know about wishes is this – you can't just wish for more wishes. Otherwise, what would be the point of someone – a genie, I suppose – saying, "I grant you three wishes"? I mean, there have to be limits to these things, right?

Everyone, when they say, "If I had three wishes, I'd wish for a thousand wishes," they think they're being clever. But it isn't clever at all. It's obvious.

And anyway, you don't need more wishes. Everyone has wishes. You need more magic – that's the stuff that's in short supply.

Think of it like bread and butter – if you have too much of one and not enough of the other, then you're going to be eating an awful lot of dry toast. Which is to say, without enough magic, you're going to end up with a whole lot of un-granted wishes.

Six months ago, if a genie had offered me three wishes, this is what I would have wished:

Wish Number 1: I wish my mum didn't have the sickness that makes her sad.

Wish Number 2: I wish I had a dog.

Wish Number 3: I wish my knees were less knobbly.

But six months was a very long time ago – kind of like once upon a time, you might say. Things are different now.

I don't know exactly how wishes work. But I knew a man who did. His name was Mr Djinn. And I miss him very much.

Six months earlier...

1

Tears and Sneezes

"You can call me Hevver," says the lady.

Her name is Heather, but she pronounces it "Hevver" – as if it rhymes with "never".

With our teachers, we have to call them by their last names, but as Hevver is my emotional-support worker, I can use her first name. Probably this is to make me feel more relaxed. Like her gentle smile, her pink fluffy jumper and the way she widens her eyes while she waits for me to answer.

"Thank you, Hevver," I say. Then, realizing my mistake, "Sorry. I mean, Heather. Thank you, *Heather*."

"It's fine," Hevver says. And she smiles in a way that tells me I haven't offended her. Which is a relief because I don't want her to think I'm some kind of problem child.

Even if I did push a boy over in the playground and make him cry.

That's sort of why I'm here.

Not for pushing Terrence Hill over exactly (everyone knows he started it – he *always* starts it), but because me losing my temper, shouting and pushing boys is not the sort of thing I normally do. I was behaving "out of character," is what my teacher said. And she wanted to know why.

At home, we're going through what Dad calls a "rough patch". We've been going through it for a while. Sometimes it makes me sad, sometimes I get confused. Sometimes I even get a bit angry (just ask Terrence Hill). My emotions are all over the place.

Which is why, I suppose, my teacher thought I could use some emotional support.

Hevver leans forwards. "And how is everything at home, Phyllis?"

"You can call me Phyll," I say.

I hope this doesn't sound cheeky. Like I'm copying the way Heather says *Call me Hevver.* I just don't like the name Phyllis. It sounds like the name of someone about 111 years old. Which is 100 years older than I am.

Hevver tilts her head, waiting for an answer to her question: *How is everything at home?*

What she means is: *How is your mum?*

Mum got sad a while back, and she's been sad most of the time since.

She tries to be happy, but when she smiles it looks like it's a hard thing for her to do. *She's not well,* is what Dad says. But it's not cancer, or anything like that. It's called depression, and it can make you so sad you forget how to smile and you don't want to get out of bed. Sometimes for days.

"She still gets sad," I say to Hevver. "But she had a good day last week."

Hevver pulls a funny face. She holds one finger in the air in a way that seems to say: *Hold on a moment.* She holds her hand to her mouth, closes one eye and ... sneezes.

"Bless you," I say.

"Phew," says Hevver, brushing her hand over the fluff of her jumper. "It's this jumper. Always makes me" – she wrinkles her nose – "sneeze. Now, tell me about the good day. At home."

"Saturday," I say. "Mum was out of bed and rearranging the books. They were all over the place."

"You have a lot of books?"

"Hundreds. Mum's a writer."

"An aufor!" says Hevver. "How glamorous."

People often say this when they find out Mum is an author. But the reality is, when she's writing, her office is a mess of dirty teacups, plates of toast and piles of paper. She has ink on her fingers and at least one pencil stuck in her hair. It's certainly not my idea of glamorous.

"So," says Hevver, "she was rearranging books?"

"Mum wanted to put them in alphabetic order, by who wrote them. So me and Dad said we'd help her. It was fun."

But – I can hear it in my voice – the way I say *fun* doesn't match the meaning of the word. I say it like the memory makes me sad.

Hevver must hear it too. She smiles gently and says, "Then what happened, Phyll?"

"About halfway through sorting the books, Mum started getting a bit ... frustrated. She said instead of arranging them by author, we should sort them by title instead."

"And did you?"

I shake my head. "Dad told her it didn't matter because we'd have to do it all again soon anyway. And then they both looked at me like Dad had said something he shouldn't have."

Hevver nods. It's a *tell me more* nod.

"Mum and Dad said they had been thinking." I feel a lump in my throat and my eyes feel slippery like I might cry.

Hevver leans forwards and holds both of my hands in hers. She is so close now that the fluff of her jumper tickles my forehead.

"Thinking about what, Phyllis?"

"Phyll," I correct her.

"Sorry. Thinking of what, Phyll?"

"Thinking of moving."

What Mum and Dad said was that they thought living in a big city like we do now might not be best for Mum's depression. They said if we lived somewhere quieter – somewhere near the sea, maybe – that the peace and the nature might help Mum get better.

"And how did that make you feel?"

"Not good."

"Not good how?"

"My friends are here, my school is here, my Guides group is here."

Hevver nods. "Did you say this to your mum and dad?"

"Dad said I could always make new friends. But that we had to make a decision that was best for everybody."

"And what did you think about that?"

What I thought was that Mum and Dad had already made their minds up and there was no use talking about it any more. So I stormed out of the room, slammed the door and went up to my room and cried. Then, two days later, I pushed Terrence Hill over for pulling my hair.

But I have a feeling Hevver already knows all of this. Otherwise, what am I doing here?

Hevver reaches into her bag. "I've brought you something," she says. "Here." And she passes me a small notebook with a sparkly cover.

"A book?"

"It's for you to write down your forts," says Hevver.

It takes me a moment to get her meaning. "My *thoughts*?"

"That's right." Hevver holds out her hand and when she opens it there is a tiny key nestled in the centre of her palm. "It's got a lock."

I look at the notebook and notice the tiny padlock attached to one edge of the book, holding the pages closed.

"Anything you write in here is private. Just for you."

"Why?"

"Because writing your forts down can make them easier to understand. Easier to cope with."

"What sort of forts?" I ask.

Hevver smiles. "Any forts at all. Things that make you sad or angry. Things that make you happy or hopeful. Things that confuse or amuse you. Oh, a rhyme!"

"Confuse or amuse," I repeat.

"I know you're having a tough time," Hevver says. "But you're not alone. You can talk to your father about anything. He wants you to know that."

"Okay."

"And if something is difficult to tell your father, you can talk to me."

"And what if I can't talk to you?" I ask.

What if we move hundreds of miles away and I have no friends and Dad's at work and you're all the way down here? Who do I talk to then? I don't say, but I certainly think.

Hevver smiles and taps the cover of the notebook. "That's what this is for," she says. "It really helps."

I feel that lump in my throat again, like I'm about to cry, so I just nod and mutter "Thank you."

Hevver leans forwards and hugs me. She smells of coffee and soap, and the fluff on her jumper is tickling my nose now and I feel as if I'm going to...

I sneeze.

And it's a big one.

A *loud* one.

Dad says my sneeze sounds like a fox that's had its tail stepped on. Mum says it sounds like a man who's just whacked his thumb with a hammer. I don't know what either of those things sounds like, but when I sneeze in class everyone laughs. Except Mrs Johnson who frowns as though I've said a naughty word.

When I sneeze now, Hevver jumps back from me and yelps like she's seen a mouse. Or maybe like a fox having its tail stepped on.

"Oh my goodness," she says, putting a hand to her chest.

"Sorry," I say, "your jumper."

"Yes," says Hevver. "It is rather fluffy."

"No," I say, pointing.

Hevver looks to where I'm pointing, at the great shining blob of snot that has flown from my nose onto her jumper.

"Oh," says Hevver. "Right."

"Sorry," I say again.

"Not to worry," says Hevver producing a tissue from the sleeve of her jumper. "Happens all the time."

Fort #1

My head is full of thoughts. Or "Forts", as Hevver calls them. Sometimes they keep me awake at night. Sometimes they distract me during class and Mrs Johnson will call me "Far Away Phyllis." Which is funny when you think about it, because if we move to somewhere near the sea, that's exactly what I'll be. Far away.

But now, holding this new notebook in my hand, flicking through all the white, unwritten pages, it's hard to catch hold of just one thought. Like trying to catch a single butterfly from a cloud of tiny flapping creatures.

You reach for one, and it's gone ... slipped through your fingers.

Thoughts of my friends, school, moving house, dogs, my mum's heavy smile, Dad's sad eyes, the books still in piles where they haven't been returned to the shelves, my snot on Hevver's pink fluffy jumper.

But the thought I come back to, the one that lands now in the palm of my hand, is the way a word can mean more than one thing. Or change the way we see something.

When I asked Dad if we were definitely moving, he said

"Maybe."

Which obviously meant *yes*.

So I asked, if we did move, could I finally have a dog? And Dad said it again, "Maybe."

But this time, it meant *no*.

I call myself Phyll instead of Phyllis, because one sounds like a dusty old granny and the other sounds like me.

And I've been thinking how Hevver calls thoughts "forts". And how fort is just another word for castle. Something strong and solid. Something to protect you and keep you safe.

And I think, *yes*, my thoughts can do that too.

My thoughts can be forts.

When Hevver gave me this book, I didn't understand how writing my thoughts down was supposed to be helpful. But it's funny – writing all this down now, feels like letting go of something.

Like I'm laying down a stone, instead of carrying it around. Like I'm building something strong.

That's a good fort, I think.

That's a good place to start.

Six months later...

SUMMER

2

Trees Like Pirate Ships

My new bedroom faces west towards the sea, but you can't see the sea. To do that, you have to walk roughly 1,000 steps to get to Corsair's Cove.

According to Dad, a *corsair* is a pirate and, hundreds of years ago, pirates used this cove for all their piratey goings-on – like smuggling treasure and drinking rum. Which is how the cove got its unusual name.

1,000 steps sounds a lot, but is only about one half of a mile. At night, I can hear the waves rolling all the way from America across the Atlantic Ocean, the Celtic Sea and the Bristol Channel until they smash into the rocks on the beach 1,000 steps away.

What I can actually see from my bedroom window is an ocean of green. A vast field that rises and falls like the surface of the sea in a storm. The trees outside my window all lean towards our new house, blown that way by centuries of wind coming in over the cliffs. At night, they look like pirate ships tossed on waves.

The sun rises in the east, so it doesn't appear in my window until later in the day, heading out towards the sea and dipping below the horizon late in the evening. Even so, it's the first week of August, and my bedroom has been bright with leaked light since before seven o'clock. The room came with blue curtains printed with white stars. Dad said I could choose new ones, but there's something soothing about these, even if the stars do let a little light through.

Dad knocks on my door at one minute past eight.

"Any pirates in here?" He speaks in a whisper because Mum is still sleeping.

"Only one," I answer.

Dad comes into the room, kneels beside the bed and bundles me up in my blanket.

"Storm," he says, and he rocks me back and forth as if my bed is a ship at sea.

"Coffee and eggs in fifteen minutes," he says, kissing me on the forehead. His hair is wet from the shower, but it's easy to imagine he is drenched from ocean spray coming over the decks of our ship.

Downstairs we can talk in normal voices, because the kitchen is on the other side of the house from Mum and Dad's bedroom. While Dad serves up the eggs, he lets me make his coffee. Dad is very particular about his coffee – it has to be done *just* right, he says, otherwise it ends up tasting like swamp water. Luckily, he has a machine that does the hard work, I just need to add the right amount of coffee beans and press the right buttons.

Once the coffee is made, I add milk. Though only as much as you can pour in the time it takes to say "perfect", which I say out loud as I perform this final step.

"Yes," says Dad, like he always does, "you are."

We eat our breakfast on a wooden table in the garden, and the steam rises off Dad's coffee like an escaping cloud.

"Sip?" he says, sliding the mug towards me.

Children shouldn't drink coffee, but a sip, Dad says, won't do me any harm.

I smell it first, the way Dad does. Closing his eyes and savouring the aroma, almost as if he is tasting the coffee through his nose before he lets it near his mouth. The smell is a mixture of soil, wood and biscuits.

Which might not sound very appetising but, trust me, it smells delicious.

And it tastes even better, if I do say so myself.

"That's enough," Dad says, as I go to take a second sip.

"Just one more?"

He holds his finger close to his thumb, which is Dad's way of saying, *A small one.*

"Excited about today?" he asks.

Nervous, is how I feel, but I just nod as I swallow my coffee.

"It'll be great," Dad says. "A good chance to make some new friends."

"Sure," I say, sliding the cup back across the table.

Camp Sunshine started one week ago, but because of us only just arriving here from London, we spent last week moving into our new house, unpacking and getting to know Cliffside Village. Not that there is much to know – a few small shops, a pub, a playground, a doctor's, a pet shop and an old folks' home. There are also two schools. One where I'll be going in September, and another – a primary school – where I'll be going this morning for my first day at Camp Sunshine.

"My first day too," Dad says. "I think I'm more nervous than you."

I seriously doubt it, I don't say.

The difference between our first days is that Dad knows some of the people from his new office. I know no one at summer camp. The hope is that there will be a few children preparing for big school like me, ideally girls. But anyone friendly will be welcome.

Dad checks his watch. "Right, teeth and hair, then I'll give you a lift to camp."

"It's only a fifteen minute walk," I say. "I don't mind walking."

"You can walk tomorrow. Let your dad drop you off on your first day."

"Fine. But no embarrassing kisses in front of the other children."

Dad laughs and ruffles my hair. "I promise nothing."

Unlike London, where the houses are squashed together and stacked on top of each other, here the cottages and houses are more spread out. The nearest house to ours is a five minute walk, the second nearest a five minute run. One good change is that Dad doesn't have to travel as far to get to work any more. In London, it could take him more than an hour to get to his office, and he would usually leave the house before I was out of bed.

Now he works in a small city called Bristol, which is only half an hour away in the car. Which means I get to eat breakfast with Dad, and that's a much better way to start the day.

As we drive to summer camp, the sea ripples in the distance – blue-green and sparkling in the morning sunshine. Dad has the windows wound down, the air smells of beach and I can hear seagulls somewhere calling for their breakfast.

It's too soon to know if being by the sea is going to make Mum feel any better. Dad says the move has worn her out, and she has spent most of the last week in bed. Dad says she just needs a while to adjust. So, while Mum was adjusting, Dad and I have been organising the house, walking on the beach at Corsair's Cove and eating fish and chips a bit more than we probably should.

"Maybe Mum will be up when you get home," Dad says now, as if he can hear my thoughts.

"Yes," I say, trying my best to sound cheery. "Maybe."

"Have you got your phone?"

I pull it out of my bag and show it to him.

"I'll be home around six," Dad says. "Call me if you have any problems."

"I will. Call I mean."

The drive takes less than five minutes, and now that we're here – parked in front of the primary school – I feel so nervous my tummy gurgles.

"I know how you feel," Dad says, and it makes me laugh.

"Sure you don't want that big kiss?" he asks.

I look out of the car windows and see no children nearby. "Go on, then," I say.

Dad kisses me on the forehead and then the tip of my nose.

"Have fun," he says. "It'll be great."

3

A Chance to Shine

The leaflet for Camp Sunshine says:

Every child is a sunbeam.

Every day is a chance to shine.

Nine of us sit in a circle in the centre of a big hall, which is where the school children have their assemblies and school dinners. There is a glittery ball hanging from the ceiling, so I imagine this is where they have school discos too.

We should have two camp supervisors, but only one has turned up today and the other – Jody – is a bit flustered having to look after us all on her own. If I had to guess, I would say Jody is eighteen years old. She sat us down in a circle to play an ice-breaker game (to introduce me to the other children), but just as we were about to start, Jody's phone rang and she went outside to answer it.

"Boyfriend trouble," says a boy with a golden suntan and a seashell bracelet on his wrist.

"How'd you know?" snaps a pretty girl who looks to be about my age.

The boy shrugs.

The girl shrugs.

And that conversation seems to be over.

I try to think of something to add, a joke maybe, but I have butterflies in my tummy and the opportunity passes. No one pays any attention to me, but I still feel enormously self-conscious in this circle of silent children.

A minute passes.

Then two.

Then three.

"She's been a while," I say brightly.

A few heads turn in my direction, then quickly look away.

No eye contact is made.

Half of the children look younger than me, still young enough to attend this primary school, but it seems none of them are close friends. Each is occupied with some private activity: a boy playing with a puzzle cube, a girl reading a book, another tiny girl chewing absentmindedly at a fingernail. One boy has a bag of sweets hidden in his pocket that he clearly has no intention of sharing.

Next there is the boy with the seashell bracelet. He sits behind the nail-chewer, carefully plaiting her hair, although this occurs in silence, the boy occasionally repositioning her head as if she were a doll.

Finally, there is the girl who spoke earlier, huddled together with two others. The three of them whisper and giggle and shoot unfriendly glances at the other children.

They don't look much like sunbeams to me.

After five minutes, my boredom gets the better of my self-consciousness and I try again.

"So," I say. "Anyone going to big school in September?"

And I sit up straight and make a point of looking at each of the children in turn, even if they don't look at me. The boy with the seashell bracelet meets my eyes; he smiles a quick smile, nods, then returns to his hairdressing.

I turn to the pretty girl and ask the question with my eyes: *What about you?*

She looks at her friends and smirks. She says "*Big school?*" repeating my words in a teasing, childish voice, and then the three of them laugh.

So much for making a good first impression, Phyllis.

I check my watch. Jody has now been outside for eight minutes.

The secret sweet eater *slooooowly* slips one hand into his pocket. There is a rustling sound. Then he pretends to cough, puts his hand to his mouth and begins chewing.

"What you got there?" says the leader of the girl gang.

It's clear that she's talking to the boy with the sweets, but the boy doesn't look up. Quite the opposite, his cheeks flush red and he fixes his eyes on the floor between his feet.

"Oi, Sweets," says the girl again. "I'm talking to you."

This girl is so pretty she looks like she should be in an advert for something – shampoo, skin cream, toothpaste, eye drops, anything meant to make you look amazing.

Me, I'm not what you'd call a girly-girl. I'd rather wear dungarees than a dress, my hair is short and I don't own anything in pink. Although I do quite like things with unicorns on them. Mum says I'm beautiful. But all mothers say that, don't they?

Anyway, this girl is, like I said, very pretty. But her face does not match her voice, or the words she forms with it. Her voice is pointed, sharp and mean. Her voice is – quite simply – ugly.

"Whassamatter?" she says to the boy. "Stuffed your face so much your ears have stopped working?"

Her two friends laugh.

The other children watch closely, the way they might watch a nature documentary showing a mouse about to get eaten by a snake. Sweets looks over his shoulder. Jody is still outside talking on the phone and it's clear she won't be coming to his rescue anytime soon.

"Whassin your pocket?" says the girl.

Sweets ignores her. Slides his hand out of his pocket and places it in his lap.

"Sharing's caring," says the girl with the ugly voice. "Come on, pass 'em round."

The boy dips his head, like he's trying to make himself as small as possible, hoping his hunter will get bored and leave him be. But this isn't the kind of girl who moves on when she has a victim in her sights.

"If I have to get up and come over there," she says, "you'll proper regret it. You hear me fat ears?"

Tears form in the corners of the boy's eyes. His lower lip trembles.

I can't watch this any more.

"I'm Phyll," I say. My mouth is dry with nerves, and my name comes out a bit croaky.

I don't know why I thought I should stand while I announced my name to eight total strangers. But that is exactly what I've done, and now they are all staring at me like I'm a complete loony. But at least – for now – the girl isn't tormenting the boy any more. Which I suppose is what I was aiming for.

But now that I'm all stood up and announced, I have no idea what to do next.

So I just smile. And wave.

"Phil?" says the girl, only she makes her voice deep, like a man's. "Phil's a boy's name."

The boy with the seashell bracelet stops plaiting the little girl's hair and narrows his eyes at me; he tilts his head slightly to one side, as if trying to decide whether or not I am, in fact, a boy.

"Short for Phyllis," I say.

The boy nods, as if some mystery has been solved, then continues working on the tiny girl's hair.

Ugly Voice is still staring at me, so to fill the silence I add, "With a Y."

"With a what?"

"Y."

"Why what?" she says, stressing the question mark.

"Phyllis with a Y," I say. "P-H-Y-L-L-I-S. Phyllis."

"Oh," says the girl, all sarcastic. "He can spell."

"I'm a girl," I say.

"Could've fooled me," she says, and when she laughs her two friends laugh with her.

"I doubt that's very difficult," I manage.

"What?"

"Fooling you," I say. "I can't imagine that's a very hard thing to do."

For a second, she is too stunned to reply, her mouth falling open and her eyes going wide in disbelief. And then her mouth closes tight, her nose wrinkles and her eyebrows bunch together. I suppose you'd call it a scowl, but the word doesn't seem strong enough. Her friends look shocked, staring first at me, then at the girl; one of them shuffles a little to the side, as if Ugly Voice were a bomb that might at any moment explode.

The boy with the seashell bracelet nods at me, as if to say, *"Good one."*

Or maybe he's saying, *"Well, Phyllis, that was pretty stupid."*

This girl stares at me like I've just slapped her. And as if she'd like to slap me right back. But I stand firm and hold her gaze, even though my knees are trembling inside my dungarees.

And so much for making new friends on your first day, Phyllis with a Y.

Just as the tension becomes almost unbearable, the door rattles on its hinges and Jody walks back into the room. She looks red-faced and flustered, as if she's been arguing perhaps.

The expression of loathing vanishes from my new enemy's face and is instantly replaced with one of innocence and sweetness. It's quite impressive.

"Everything all right, Jody?" she says.

Jody has thick, curly brown hair, and she pushes her fingers into it now, shaking it out and springing it up. As if what she is really doing is shaking herself out. Springing herself up. "Fine, thank you, Hilda," she says. "Just some … personal stuff."

And now my enemy has a name: *Hilda*.

"Right," says Jody. "How about we play that ice-breaker game and welcome Phyllis to Camp Sunshine?"

Where every child is a sunbeam, I think. *And every day is a chance to shine.*

"Oh, we've already done that, haven't we, *Phil*?" says Hilda.

Obviously Phyll and Phil sound exactly the same, but I can tell by the look on Hilda's face that she is spelling my name the boys' way.

"Oh," says Jody, "you've already made some friends. Lovely. Right, who wants to play dodgeball?"

The answer to Jody's question is: *hardly anyone.*

The younger children look at the ground, the boy with the seashell bracelet sighs, and I don't even know what dodgeball is, although I have a horrible suspicion it involves having balls thrown at you.

Hilda, on the other hand, is very keen to play and she says so several times in her loud and pointed voice. And, as she is the only one talking, she is the only one who is listened to.

"Great," says Jody. "Dodgeball it is."

4

The Floor Rushes Up to Meet Me

My suspicions were correct.

Dodgeball does involve having balls thrown at you.

Jody attempts to explain the rules, but explaining does not appear to be one of her strong points. Fortunately, the game is simple. There are two teams and four balls. You throw the balls at each other. If you hit someone they're out. There were other rules, but no one could agree on what these were.

"Right," says Jody, clapping her hands. "Two teams."

Hilda, who is already in a huddle with her friends, puts her hand up. "Can Phil be on our team please, Jody?"

Jody shrugs. "Don't see why not."

Hilda smiles. It's a rather sinister smile.

I was sure she would want me on the *opposite* team. Giving her, and her giggling friends, plenty of opportunity to knock my head off with a dodgeball. So this turn of events is a little confusing.

Jody sends the two teams to opposite ends of the school gymnasium.

On one side: me, Hilda and her friends.

On the other: everybody else.

Jody holds the whistle to her lips ... and blows.

We sprint towards the balls. Well my team does, the other team just stand where they are, as if whatever happens next is somehow inevitable. Like sheep waiting to be sheared. Or skittles waiting to be knocked down.

They are completely relaxed at the prospect of being pelted with dodgeballs.

And then I realize why.

The balls are made from red sponge – and far from being able to knock anyone's head off, it's unlikely they could even mess up your hair.

"Throw it!" shouts Hilda, while she and her friends launch their own balls at the opposite team. I'm standing directly opposite the boy with the bracelet, so it seems only fair that I aim at him.

It's a good shot, but the boy leans casually to his left and the ball sails past his ear, missing him by millimetres. He raises an eyebrow at me as if to say, *Nice try.*

Or maybe it's, *So you're one of them now, are you?*

It's hard to tell.

After five minutes of play, my team has lost one player, the other team has lost two, and I'm amazed to find that I'm enjoying myself. I'm also beginning to think Hilda might not be quite so awful as I'd first assumed. Yes, she was horrible to Sweets, but maybe she'd had a bad morning. Perhaps she and Sweets have a long-running feud. Maybe there is something else troubling her. As Dad always says – *Don't be quick to judge other people, otherwise other people might be quick to judge you.*

The balls are scattered far and wide, so Jody blows her whistle and lines them up again in the centre of the hall. Both teams take their places at opposite sides of the gym. I fix my eyes on one of the balls, bend my knees and lean forwards like a sprinter in a race.

Jody blows her whistle.

And I'm off, the soles of my trainers squeaking on the wooden floor as I run towards the ball at full speed. The boy with the bracelet is going for the same ball, but he doesn't stand a chance.

I reach down, and I'm just about to snatch the ball, when I feel something connect with my back foot and the floor comes rushing up to meet me.

Bang!

I land hard on my chest and tummy, knocking most of the air out of my body. My head connects with the floor a split second after the rest of me. I see stars, and when my vision clears, everyone is standing around me in a circle.

Jody's face is set in an expression of high alarm. "Are you okay?"

I put my hand to my forehead and wince when my fingers find a bump, but – much to my surprise – no blood.

"I'm fine," I say, pushing myself into a sitting position.

"I think you might have cracked the floor," says the boy with the seashell bracelet. He's smiling, but not in an unkind way. More like he is somehow impressed.

"Must have slipped," I say.

And then I see Hilda. She is smiling too, but this is not a friendly smile. This smile is mean and cold and very pleased with itself. As I clamber to my feet, Hilda takes a step back from the group so that only I can see her. She points to her outstretched foot, points to me, then points at the floor. And then she winks.

She tripped me.

That's why she wanted me on her team. She knew she couldn't hurt me with a sponge dodgeball; much better to have me on her team where she could send me crashing to the floor.

"Let's get an ice pack on that head," says Jody. "Clark," she says to the boy with the bracelet, "fetch one from the nurse's office, would you?"

"I'm fine," I say to Jody.

"Could have fooled me," says Hilda. "Then again, I can't imagine that's a very hard thing to do."

The exact same words I said to her earlier.

Hilda smiles once more, turns and skips away.

And sometimes, it seems, your first impressions are right, after all.

5

Yell and Tell

The bump on my head was not as bad as I first thought, and you can't even see it if I smooth my short fringe forwards. But for the rest of the day (with Jody being nervous about breaking any more children, I suppose) we spent our time inside doing less dangerous activities like painting, decorating biscuits and playing board games. Or "boring games" as Clark, the boy with the bracelet, calls them.

I didn't mind the games so much, but as I walk home from Camp Sunshine, my legs are restless and I have an urge to feel the cold waves washing over my feet. And maybe to find some pretty shells.

There are two ways onto Corsair's Cove.

The first way is down a long and winding path. Mostly the path is made of gradually sloping sand that is occasionally so steep you feel like you might tumble forwards. In some parts, there are wooden boards bedded into the sand and, closer to the beach itself, there is a stretch of stone steps that look like they could be a staircase in a castle or a fortress.

This is not a beach you just wander onto. Visiting Corsair's Cove takes commitment, Dad says, and today I count 461 steps before I reach the soft sand.

The second way onto the cove is to fall. This would be much quicker than walking down the long and winding path, but I doubt it would be very beneficial for your health.

Looking from above, the beach is surrounded by cliffs and shaped like a hoofprint. As if some giant monster had climbed out of the sea and stamped its foot through the cliffs on its way to wherever giant sea monsters go.

The beach is beautiful, the sand is clean and there aren't many people down here. (On account of the long path, probably.) I count seven people and three dogs. One dog walks beside its owner, another chases after a ball and the third – a big, shaggy-furred thing – barks excitedly as it runs in and out of the waves.

This must be a good place to be a dog. A good place to *have* a dog.

I would give all my Christmas and birthday presents for the next ten years to have a dog. Maybe even all my Christmas presents and birthday presents for ever.

But when I said this to Dad he'd smiled the way grown-ups do when they know they're going to disappoint you.

"*Let's wait and see*," he'd said.

Which is just another way of saying *no*.

Halfway between the sea and the cliffs, there is a dark line of seaweed, which must have been washed out there by the tide. It stretches from one end of the cove all the way to the other and I walk this line as if it were a tightrope, with my arms stretched out for balance.

If I half close my eyes, I can imagine that the sand is 100 metres below me and that a single slip will plunge me to my peril.

I'm halfway across when a voice startles me.

"Careful," it says. "You don't want to fall."

I'm so involved in my game of make-believe that I stumble and one foot steps wide of the line. I look around for the source of this voice and see a man watching me.

"Oops," he says. "Too late."

He laughs when he says it, and smiles, but something about him makes me feel uneasy. Maybe it's because he wears sunglasses and I can't see his eyes. Maybe it's his beard – one of those little ones that television baddies have. Or maybe I'm simply jumpy because I almost fell to my death from a 100-metre-high tightrope.

"Local?" the man says.

We had a talk at school about *Stranger Danger*.

Basically, mostly everyone in the world is a stranger. Fortunately, most people are good. But there are bad people out there that might try and harm you. To stay safe from strangers, you need to avoid dangerous places where you might be alone – like a forest, or dark alleyways. Public places are best and I'm glad of the other people here now.

"Beautiful beach, isn't it?" says the man.

I nod.

Warning signs of a bad stranger are strangers that offer you sweets or money and strangers that ask you to go anywhere with them or get in a car. You should also be careful of strangers that ask lots of questions.

"Don't talk much, do you?" says the man.

I shrug.

In school they told us that if a stranger tries to approach you, then you take four big steps backwards. If they still try to come towards you, the teacher told us to shout "No!". To shout it as loud as we possibly could. We practised in the playground – taking it in turns to scream "No!" at the top of our lungs.

We all found it very funny.

But now, standing in front of this stranger with his baddie-beard, it doesn't feel so funny.

"Yell and tell" the teacher called it. Because after yelling "No!" and running away, you are supposed to tell a grown-up.

But this man doesn't try and approach me. He hasn't offered me anything and he hasn't asked me to go anywhere with him.

All the same, I'd like him to leave now.

Behind the man, I see two people walking down the path towards the beach. Without even thinking about it, I wave in their direction as if I know them. The man turns to look where I'm waving.

I think about running towards the people, even though they are strangers too, but then I notice that the man is holding a dog lead. Maybe he is the owner of the big shaggy beast that likes to run into the waves. Maybe he's not a bad person after all.

The man sees that I have spotted the lead and jangles it in his hand as if only then remembering he's holding it. "Best be off," he says. "You have a nice day – and be careful on that tightrope."

He does a short wave, then turns and heads off towards the steps.

I say goodbye under my breath, but the man doesn't hear it against the breeze coming in off the sea.

6

A Lost Dog

Mum – before everything went wonky – used to drop me off and pick me up from school in the car. And sometimes Mum, Dad and me would go for a walk at the weekend. But not often.

The point is, my legs aren't used to this much walking and what with all the steps down to and up from the beach, they're tired as I walk home. It's a good tired, though, and if nothing else, maybe moving here means I'll get some muscles on my legs. Not too much, hopefully, not like a rugby player or anything, but enough so my knees aren't quite so knobbly.

"Like knots in a pair of bootlaces," Dad says.

There's a bench on the side of the road, so I sit down to empty what feels like half of the beach out of my trainers. The sand forms two small heaps and I push it around with my feet, flattening it and tracing shapes with my toes. I tilt my face upwards to feel the sun, which is still high even though it's almost suppertime.

And there, floating above me, is the face of the cutest dog imaginable. Except this is a *picture* of a dog rather than a dog itself.

LOST DOG says the poster stapled to the lamppost.

In the picture, the dog's tongue is hanging out and its eyes are wide and bright. I know this breed – it's a Yorkshire terrier; tiny, fluffy and with high pointed ears like a cuddly toy. The way the hair falls on its face makes it look like it has a moustache and bushy eyebrows. It is adorable.

And it's so, so sad at the same time.

According to the poster, the dog is called Tim.

The poster says: *TIM IS A GENTLE DOG, AND WE ARE VERY WORRIED ABOUT HIM. A REWARD IS OFFERED FOR ANY INFORMATION LEADING TO HIS SAFE RETURN.*

I can't imagine anything more miserable than being the owner of a lost dog. It must feel worse than never having had a dog at all. I take my phone out of my bag and enter the number printed on the bottom of the poster. The owner hasn't put their name on the poster, so I save the number with the dog's name – just in case I spot him.

Just in case I can be the one to save him.

Then I put my trainers back on and head for home.

7

Lost Rubbers and Other Clouds

You don't get to be almost twelve years old without having your fair share of drama.

I had my favourite rubber that smelled of pineapple stolen. I've been not invited to a birthday party by someone I thought was a friend. I've had my hair pulled, I've had a BFF dump me for someone else and I've been teased about my mermaid bathing costume in swimming lessons.

I've had tough times, all right.

And I can certainly cope with Hilda.

The trick is not to take this stuff personally. It's not that there's anything wrong with *you*. It's them – the hair-pullers, the rubber thieves, the name-callers – that have the problem. The trick is to ignore it, put it behind you and move on.

I know all of this because my mum told me so.

I don't *need* any emotional support.

But I would still like to tell Mum about my disastrous first day at Camp Sunshine. So she can sit me on her knee and stroke my hair and tell me that everything will be okay. Because when she says it, it sounds more believable than when I say it to myself.

Maybe Dad was right; maybe Mum will be feeling better today.

Walking home, I let myself picture Mum sitting in her office, a pencil tucked into her hair as she taps away on her computer, writing the first chapter of a brand-new story. When Mum used to write, she would often sing to herself in her office and you could hear her voice in all the rooms of the house. Her voice isn't very good, but I miss the sound of her singing all the same.

Dad describes the way Mum feels when her depression is bad as living under a cloud. "You can't just make a cloud vanish," he says. "You just have to hope that one day it will blow over."

Maybe today, I tell myself. *Maybe today the sea air and the gentle breeze has blown the cloud away.*

As I approach the house, I imagine hearing Mum sing as I put my key in the front door. Imagine her stopping when she hears me walk into the house.

Imagine her calling down the stairs, "Hey Hedgehog, how was your day?"

And when I tell her, Mum will ruffle my hair, kiss the bump on my forehead and say to me, "Good job you're such a tough little critter, isn't it?"

Then maybe I'll read on the floor of her office while she carries on working.

But as I push my key into the lock and open the door, the house is dark and quiet.

Mum is not reading a book in the kitchen or scribbling notes for a story.

She is not singing in her office.

And I can feel the cloud as if it were a real thing, filling the house and casting its dark shadow over the walls, the furniture and me.

Fort #46

Dad says that when I was born, my eyes were small and squinched closed, and I had thick, spiky brown hair. Mum said I looked like a hedgehog and, because they hadn't decided on a name for me yet, that's what they called me before they called me anything else. I was Hedgehog for five whole days before I was Phyllis.

They still call me Hedgehog more than they call me by my real name. Which is fine by me.

Whenever we have spaghetti, it's "Eat your worms, Hedgehog."

Or if my hair's messy (which it usually is), it's "Brush your spikes, Hedgehog."

And at night, after reading me a story, Mum would tuck me into my blankets, kiss my nose and say "Happy Hibernating, Hedgehog."

But I realized something today. Mum hasn't tucked me into bed once since we moved here – and I can't remember her calling me Hedgehog for a long time either. As if the part of her that writes stories, sings badly and reads to me at bedtime – her Happy, I suppose you could call it – is lost.

Like the dog on the poster.

Or maybe it's only hibernating.

I like this idea more.

When something is lost, it might be lost for ever. But hibernation is a not-for-ever thing. Hibernation always ends sooner or later. You just have to be patient and wait for the weather to change. You have to wait for the clouds to blow over.

8

Camp Downpour

There are nine children at Camp Sunshine, but on my first day, my main feeling (apart from the feeling of a massive bump on my head) was of being alone. Now, though, that feeling has blown away. All it took was a single friend. Even if he is a boy.

By the end of my first week, I have learned everybody's name and we have settled into three groups:

Hilda and her two friends, who I now think of as Hilda and the Horribles.

The younger children, who I have imaginatively named The Youngsters.

And me and Clark – the boy with the seashell bracelet.

The boys at my old school had two favourite things to do:

1) Play football

2) Annoy girls

Maybe it's just a local thing but – so far, at least –

Clark hasn't mentioned football or pulled my hair once. I wouldn't go as far as to say we're *best* friends. But I think we could be.

Jody and the other supervisor, Harriet, organise games and activities, but mostly me and Clark spend our time as a twosome, drawing, talking and working our way through Camp Sunshine's collection of "boring games". It turns out Clark and I both have birthdays in November and we will be starting at the same high school at the end of the summer holidays.

We have fun, but I don't know if our friendship will survive when we start at our new school – what with me being a girl and him being a boy. Annoyingly, Hilda and the Horribles will also be starting Year 7 in September and I can already hear Hilda's awful teasing voice:

Phyll and Clark up a tree, K-I-S-S-I-N-G.

Even the idea of it makes me blush.

"You OK, Phyll?"

"What?"

Clark is giving me a strange look. We're sitting outside, hiding from the heat under the shade of a wide palm tree, playing snakes and ladders but not really concentrating too much on the game.

"I'm fine," I say, picking up the dice.

"Your face has gone red."

"It's hot," I tell him, "in case you hadn't noticed."

"Yeah, but it's gone *really* red."

Obviously I can't tell Clark what I was thinking, so I bring up something else that's been on my mind.

"Why is it that Hilda gets tongue-tied when you stand up to her?" I say. "She's not like that with me."

"How'd you mean?"

"Take that Hitler thing, for example."

"Oh, yeah," says Clark, laughing. "The Hitler thing."

The Hitler thing:

It was Wednesday, and Jody was trying to get Hilda and the Horribles to play outside instead of sitting indoors all day and painting each other's nails.

"No thanks," said Hilda.

"Come on," said Jody. "The sun'll do you some good."

"What," said Hilda, "and get freckles?" And she smirked at me when she said it.

I have *tons* of freckles.

"What's wrong with freckles?" I said.

"Nothing," Hilda said, "if you want to be *ordinary*. My mother says I'm going to be famous. So I need to protect my delicate skin from sun damage."

"Famous what?" I asked.

Hilda scowled at me. "What are you on about now, *Philip*?"

"You said you were going to be famous. A famous what?"

Hilda sighed like this was a stupid question. "Doesn't matter. Singer, model, actress, whatever. Famous is famous. You've either got it or you've not. And – unlike some, *Philip* – I've got it."

"Hitler was famous," said Clark.

And I wonder if Hilda is aware of the similarity between her name and that of the infamous Nazi war criminal.

For someone so quick to tease, sneer, name-call and generally use her mouth as a weapon, Hilda doesn't seem so sure of herself when she's dealing with Clark. Her brow furrowed and her lips moved silently as she tried – and failed – to think of a clever comeback.

I almost felt sorry for her.

"At least you know who he is," she said after some considerable effort.

Then Adolf Hilda and her horrible friends swaggered away to paint each other's nails.

Sitting with Clark now, I say to him, "If I'd said that, she would have said something completely mean right back at me. But with you she just goes all … daft."

"Well," says Clark, pushing his fringe out of his eyes, which are, now that I look into them, incredibly blue. Blue like the sky. "She has a crush on me."

"She what?"

This news makes me feel strange. I feel ... not jealous. Definitely not that. Obviously. But ... I don't know ... strange.

"You've gone red again," says Clark.

"It's still hot."

Clark looks at me carefully for a moment then shrugs. "Fair enough."

"How do you know?" I say. "That she has a crush on you?"

"I can just tell."

"Really?"

He nods. "And one of her friends told me."

"So ... what did you say?"

Clark laughs. "I said I already had a girlfriend."

Again, I get a strange feeling that is absolutely definitely not jealousy.

"Is she going to our new school?" I ask. "This ... girlfriend?"

"I doubt it," says Clark. "She doesn't exist."

"Doesn't exist," I say, and, if I didn't know better, I'd say I sounded relieved.

"Seemed like the easiest way of dealing with Hilda," says Clark.

"Oh, you're crafty," I tell him. "Very, very crafty."

"I know," says Clark, and when he laughs, I laugh too.

And then the weather changes.

Really changes.

There is a bang of thunder. I actually yelp, but the sound is drowned out by more thunder – a loud tearing sound, as if the sky itself is being torn open. Black clouds roll in overhead and I shiver against the sudden cold. Lightning flashes against the dark clouds, splitting and branching as it shoots towards the earth. I've never seen anything like it – it's beautiful and magnificent and absolutely terrifying. The lightning is followed by another crack of thunder.

Then the rain comes. Freezing cold drops as fat as jellybeans explode downwards, rattling on the leaves and bouncing off the ground. And even under the palm tree, we are instantly soaked.

Clark shouts, "Run!"

And he doesn't need to say it twice.

"You have two choices," Jody says once we are all assembled inside. "Stay here and make papier-mâché with me..."

"*Or…*" says Harriet, drawing out the suspense like she's about to announce the most awesome activity ever, "you can visit the old folks' home with me!"

The truth is, I'd *much* rather make papier-mâché. But I feel bad for Harriet, who is looking at us expectantly with an expression like a puppy waiting for a walk.

It's a real dilemma.

Until…

"Papier-mâché for me, please," says Hilda in the voice she always uses when she's trying to pretend to Jody that she's not the most horrible girl in the world. "Right, girls?" says Hilda, turning to her Horribles. You can see in her eyes that she's not asking, she's telling.

"Right," say the Horribles obediently.

And my mind is made up.

"I'll go to the old folks' home," I say.

"Brilliant!" says Harriet. "Anyone else?"

And it seems I'm not the only one who would rather do anything at all than hang around with Hilda, the Horribles and a bucket full of soggy paper.

"Sure," says Clark. "I'll go."

And the rest of the youngsters say they'll come too.

Harriet is delighted.

9
The Genie

Because of the rain, Harriet drives us to Ocean Breeze old folks' home in a minibus, even though the journey takes only three minutes. The home is a glass-fronted building set a short way back from the cliff's edge and surrounded by neat green lawns. The gardens offer a spectacular view of the sea and, if it wasn't for the sturdy white fence, it would be easy for a careless old folk to wander off the edge and into a very long drop.

When we walk into the living room, several residents turn to see who has arrived. Some look pleased to see us, others regard us with a mixture of bewilderment and suspicion. The room is as big as the school canteen, but everywhere there are armchairs, wooden chairs, sofas and tables.

Music plays from speakers that are screwed high to the walls. I don't recognize any of the songs, but some of the old folk are doing their best to sing along and two elderly ladies dance slowly beneath one of the speakers.

At one table a pair of old men play dominoes. At another a lady is colouring in the squares of a crossword puzzle. Some sit alone, others sit and mutter to each other. Or to themselves.

"Well," says Harriet, "what are you all waiting for? Go and talk to someone."

One by one, the other children drift into the room and take seats next to waiting ladies and gentlemen. Several old folk are still watching me and I worry that whoever I sit with, I will offend those that I leave out. Maybe I stand there too long because, gradually, the old faces turn away from me. All except one.

The man's brown skin is criss-crossed with wrinkles and his white hair is tied in a neat ponytail. If he had an eye patch he'd look exactly like a pirate.

The man tilts his head to the side, as if to say, *Are you coming, or what?* And, even at this distance, his eyes sparkle with amusement. As if he knows something that I don't. He smiles as I walk towards him and, as I draw close, he extends a thin arm and pats the back of the chair beside his.

"Thank you," he says. His voice is slow and low and he speaks with an accent that I can't place. "Please, sit."

I do as he asks and the chair creaks beneath me. Between us is a small table on which is a steaming cup of what might be tea or coffee, and a thick book with the title *Tales from 1001 Nights*. The book cover shows two men on a flying carpet, floating over rooftops that are shaped like giant swirls of ice cream.

"I'm Phyll," I say.

"Phil?" says the man, leaning forwards in his chair.

"It's short for Phyllis," I tell him, "but—"

"But … you don't feel like a Phyllis?"

"No," I say, not freaked out exactly, but more than a little intrigued. "How did you know?"

The man smiles gently. "I pay attention," he says. "For example, when a girl called Phyllis introduces herself as Phyll, it's only sensible to assume she doesn't like her given name. Even if it is a beautiful one."

Normally, a comment like that would make me blush. But the way this man says it – as if he is simply commenting on the colour of my shoes – I don't feel at all embarrassed.

"It's a good trick," I say.

The man bows his head. "You don't get to be my age without learning a trick or two."

I look at his creased skin and pure white hair and wonder just how old he is. The wrinkles are so deep in places that they could hide a matchstick, but his hair is thick and glossy in a way that old people's normally isn't. His hands are thin and they shake slightly, but his eyes look like those of a much younger person. I notice, too, that he wears a hooped gold earring in one ear.

"I'm eleven," I tell him, and the man seems to find this rather funny. "Why are you laughing?"

"Because what you really wanted to do was ask how old I am. But you're too polite, so you told me your age instead. Am I right?"

And – now that I think of it – he is right. Although I hadn't realized that's what I was doing.

"Guess," the man says. "Guess my age within ten years and you can have a biscuit." He nods to the table in front of him where there is a packet of chocolate-chip cookies that I hadn't noticed when I sat down.

"Okay, I guess you are ... seventy-seven."

The man shakes his head, flicks his eyes upwards: *higher.*

"Eighty..."

Again with his eyes: *higher still.*

"Ninety! You don't look like you're in your nineties."

"I'm not," he says, lowering his voice. "I'm in my thousands."

"Thousands?"

The man nods. "And several of them, although I can't remember the exact number or when my birthday is, except that it's sometime in summer." And with that he huffs out a short laugh and leans back in his chair. "Take one," he says, nodding at the biscuits.

"But I didn't guess right."

"No. But I am feeling generous, please take one."

Lately, my granddad has been having what Mum calls "dementia", which is when someone's brain goes wonky. Because of his dementia, Granddad sometimes forgets Mum's name, which makes her cry. And he once got mustard confused with peanut butter when he was making a sandwich, which made Dad laugh, even though he said he shouldn't. According to Mum, lots of old people catch dementia, and I wonder if this man – who can't remember when his birthday is – has it too.

The man dips his biscuit in his drink, then takes a bite. "Care for a dip?"

"In your tea?"

"It's coffee," he says. "Although not very good coffee. I don't drink it, but the cup is nice to warm my hands on. And it's something with which to wet a biscuit."

He nods at the cup, encouraging me to dunk my biscuit.

And so I do.

"You can call me Djinn," he says, "with a silent *D*. It's short for Djinni, also with a silent *D*."

"Is that a first name or a last name?" I ask.

"It is an old name," he answers, but this is not really an answer at all.

"Mr Djinn," I say, trying out the sound of this soft and unusual name.

"The 'mister' is not necessary," he says. "But ... as you wish." He takes a bite of his biscuit then carefully brushes crumbs from his white moustache. "Hard to believe, isn't it?" he says.

"What is?"

"That I was alive in a time before computers, before aeroplanes and cars, before electricity and medicine and windows made of glass. Before, even, chocolate biscuits."

"It is rather ... unusual," I say, trying to be polite. After all, this man may have dementia.

"And I don't have dementia," he says, with a knowing smile.

"I didn't say—"

"No," says Mr Djinn. "You are too polite. But I believe we were discussing belief."

"Oh, were we? Right."

"Belief is a tricky thing," says Mr Djinn. "It fades and shifts and changes shape. And this can make belief hard to hold onto. What we believe changes with our age," he says. "It changes with the times. Thousands of years ago, everybody – children *and* adults – believed in magic, believed in spells, in witches and spirits. In genies."

"Like in *Aladdin*?" I say. "In the lamp?"

"I always liked him," says Mr Djinn. "A mischievous fellow to be sure, but he had a good heart."

The old man raises his cup of not very good coffee and blows on the surface, sending a coil of steam towards my face. The aroma, when it reaches my nose, smells like something more than coffee – it smells of campfires and sand and spices.

Mr Djinn sets down his coffee cup without taking a drink. He leans forwards as if he is about to share a secret. "Do you know why people believed in genies?"

I shake my head.

"Because they were *real*, child. Because *magic* is real."

"Don't people believe in genies now?" I ask.

"Do you?"

He sees me hesitate and continues.

"People don't believe in genies because they don't need them. They have rockets that can fly to the moon, computers they wear on their wrist; they have movie stars and celebrities. This is where people look for magic now, and so" – he shrugs – "they have forgotten about the likes of me."

My mind makes a connection – between the word *genie* and the name Djinn. Short for *Djinni*, said the man, and pronounced with a silent *D*.

Djinni. Genie.

"Are you saying…" Mr Djinn smiles as he waits for me to complete my question, "…that you're a genie?"

"Yes," says Mr Djinn, clapping his hands together. "That is precisely what I am saying."

I don't know what it is, but I feel an … an *energy* from Mr Djinn. He seems clever and honest and not at all like his brain has gone wonky. He feels *different*. But a genie? That's just bonkers.

"You don't believe me," he says. And it may or may not be a question.

But as I consider his words, I realize two things.

The first is that I don't know whether I believe him or not. Mostly, I absolutely don't. But a tiny voice, deep inside my head, whispers two small and exciting words: *why not?*

The second thing I realize is that it doesn't matter. That it is more fun and interesting – for me and for Mr Djinn – to go along with the idea.

"Can you grant wishes?" I ask.

Mr Djinn chuckles gently. "I am old," he says. "My knees are not so good, my back aches and I get tired. Once I could run as fast as a horse, but now, to walk further than the length of this room I require a chair with wheels. My memory, too, is not as clear as it once was. But I remember enough. I wake in the night three times to go to the toilet, not that you need to know, but it's a thing that happens when you move beyond a certain age. For most people this is around sixty; for me, it was somewhere between two and three thousand. But the end result is the same: we fade, we lose our strength and our powers as we reach the end."

"The end? The end of what?"

"This will be my last summer," says Mr Djinn. "Luckily, it is shaping up to be a most pleasant one."

I feel suddenly sad and alarmed. "You mean ... you don't mean...?"

Mr Djinn takes my hand in his. He nods. "Everything must come to an end, child. I have lived a long and wonderful life, but I am tired now and my time is near."

"But—"

"But," says Mr Djinn, and he pauses, waiting, it seems, to satisfy himself that I am paying attention, "we were not talking of ends. We were talking of wishes."

"Yes," I say. "Wishes."

The old man brightens at the word, his eyes sparkling like clear glass in sunshine. "Once," he says, "I could snap my fingers and summon into being gold, a castle, an elephant. Now it is not so easy. If it were easy, I would grant you three wishes in the click of a finger."

And then he clicks his long brown fingers – the sound is loud and crisp and it sends a shiver down the back of my neck.

Mr Djinn holds my gaze for a long (but not uncomfortable) moment, then he blinks, smiles and shifts in his chair. He pushes his fingers down the side of the cushion, his face furrows in concentration, and when his hand emerges from the chair he is holding a pack of cards. "Do you know how to play cribbage, Phyllis?"

I shake my head.

"It's the greatest card game two people can play," says Mr Djinn. "Trust me, I've played them all."

"I've never played it," I tell him.

Mr Djinn removes the cards from the box and begins to deal. "Then I will teach you."

10

Like a Treasure Hunt

The new house has more rooms than we are used to, and some of them still stand empty, patiently waiting for us to decide what to do with them.

We have three bedrooms upstairs – one for me, one for Mum and Dad, and another in case anyone wants to sleep over. There is also a study upstairs, which hopefully Mum will use to write books again, once she is feeling better.

She used to write every day, even on Sundays, even on her birthday. Even if it was only for fifteen minutes, Mum would sit at her desk and write something. And she read to me almost as often; if not every day, then certainly most, doing all the voices and actions and even roaring or shouting or shrieking if that's what the story called for. But I can't remember the last time she read me a bedtime story. Not since we moved here, that's for sure.

Downstairs in our new house, as well as the kitchen, we have a dining room plus two others. One of these –

the one we're in now – might one day be a library-type room. Somewhere to sit and read and drink cups of tea, be quiet and maybe do jigsaws without taking up the whole kitchen table.

But, for now, it is simply a room with no curtains, no shelves, no chairs. The only thing it contains – apart from us – is a bunch of boxes. And the only things they contain are books.

The box we are unpacking now is almost as tall as me. We have only halfway emptied it and already the books are spread around us in uneven heaps, piles and teetering stacks.

"We should have packed them alphabetically," Mum says.

"Probably," says Dad. He is bent at the waist and leaning into the box so his voice is muffled through cardboard.

"Might have helped us find this damn book," Mum says and, for a dreadful moment, I think she is upset about something – about the way we packed the books from our old house.

But when I look over at her she's smiling. She holds a book in each hand but neither of them is the one we're looking for. "Still," she says, "this is sort of fun though, isn't it? Like a..." She picks up another book from the pile at her feet: *Treasure Island* by someone called Robert Louis Stevenson. "Like a treasure hunt," Mum says. And her smile when she says it is a good one.

I feel especially happy, because it seems to me like I'm responsible for this smile. Like I – with maybe a little help from Mr Djinn – made it happen.

Mum slept late again today and, when we heard her moving about upstairs, Dad sent me up with a cup of tea. Mum asked about my week at camp, so I told her all of the good parts. And then – the thought popping into my head like a bird into a tree – I asked if we had the book *Aladdin*.

"Kind of," Mum had told me, and she'd explained how *Aladdin* is just one story in a much bigger book called *Tales from 1001 Nights*.

Which is exactly the same book that was on Mr Djinn's little table.

So I told Mum about Mr Djinn – that he looked like an old pirate, that he probably had dementia, and that he'd been reading *Tales from 1001 Nights*.

And Mum had said, in that case, we should unpack our books and find our own copy straight away.

Rummaging through the books now, Mum is so clearly happy. She seems lively, bright and more ... awake, I suppose, than she has been since we moved here.

Dad emerges from the box clutching another armful of paperbacks. "Maybe Mr Djinn will read you his copy."

Mum gives Dad a look that's hard to read. Like she doesn't approve of his suggestion, perhaps.

"What?" Dad says.

"Well, some of the other stories are a bit…" She waggles her hand up and down, but I have no idea what this means.

"A bit what?" I ask.

"A bit grown-up," Mum says.

"Grown-up how?"

"Oh just … Mummy and Daddy stuff."

"You mean sex?"

Mum's face reddens. "Yes, I suppose I do. And, if my memory serves, I'm not sure the women are treated very well. Not exactly suitable reading for an eleven-year-old girl."

"So why," Dad says, "am I giving myself paper cuts hunting for an 'unsuitable' book?"

"Because … I don't know, because … what's the point in having all these books if we're going to keep them all in boxes?"

"I've been busy," Dad says. "I haven't exactly had a lot of spare time to unpack everything."

"I know," Mum says, sighing. "I'm ... I'm sorry. I'm just tired."

Mum has gone still, sitting cross-legged on the floor and staring at the books around her feet, and suddenly this whole treasure hunt doesn't seem so much fun any more.

I remember the day when we were arranging the books in our old flat and how that all turned into a disaster with Mum and Dad arguing. And I'm desperate for that not to happen again.

Only a few minutes ago I felt so pleased with myself, but now it seems like everything is about to go wrong again, and if it does it will be my fault. My stomach feels uncomfortable, as if I'm standing on the deck of a ship that might at any moment capsize and send us all into the waves.

Dad smiles at me as if he feels it too and I just wish – I wish with all my heart – that this cloud would pass and our ship would settle. And as the thought passes through my mind, a shiver runs up my back.

I stand and shake out my arms, wriggling my hips and stretching my legs to shoo away the shiver. In front of me is a stack of three smallish boxes, one on top of the other. I pick up the one from the top, but as I do, the bottom of the box collapses. It pops open and spills books all over the floor, so that I am left holding nothing but an empty cardboard box.

"Oops," says Dad.

"Ha!" says Mum, reaching into the pile and picking up a thick book. The cover shows a picture of two men seated on a flying carpet, high above buildings with rounded roofs and pointed spires shaped like twists of ice cream.

It is exactly the same as the cover on Mr Djinn's copy of *Tales from 1001 Nights*.

"Weird," Mum says. "I thought it had a different cover." And then she shrugs.

"So you're going to read it?" Dad says.

Mum inspects the cover, as if she were inspecting an avocado in the supermarket, checking to see if it's ripe. "Probably not," she says.

"Now you tell me," says Dad, sweeping his hand around the room full of unpacked books. But he is smiling when he says it.

Mum laughs. "I said I wanted to *find* it. I didn't say anything about reading it."

She puts *1001 Nights* down and instead picks up the copy of *Treasure Island*.

"I was eleven when I first read this," she says. "I remember it clearly."

"Same age as me," I say.

"Same age as you."

At bedtime, Mum and Dad tuck me in together for the first time since we moved here.

I have a giant beanbag in my room. It's not quite big enough for both of them, but they somehow manage to squeeze onto it and, once they are settled Mum – with her head resting on Dad's shoulder – opens up the copy of *Treasure Island*.

"'Part One'," Mum reads. "'The Old Buccaneer'…"

As I listen to her tell the story, I watch her face. I watch her eyes track the words across the page, and I watch her smile reach all the way up to her eyes.

11

Fluttering

Today at Camp Sunshine we have come to the cove, which is a good thing and bad. Good because I love it here. Bad because I'd rather not share it with Hilda and her Horribles.

But it's mostly good. The Horribles are off doing their own thing. While me and Clark do ours. Which is walking the line of seaweed and driftwood that divides the beach in two, our eyes following our feet as we search the sand for seashells.

Clark is better at this than me, spotting all kinds of suitable shells – undamaged and neither too big nor too small. He tells me their names as he gathers them into a striped cotton bag: clams, cockles, limpets, periwinkles, button tops.

He stoops now to pick up another.

"These are Mum's favourite," he says. "It's a tiger cowrie shell. Which is weird because it's got spots not stripes. See?"

He passes the shell to me and I turn it over in my hand. The underside of the shell is pure white, with a small opening like a mouthful of tiny sharp teeth. Perhaps, if you squinted, they could even be a tiger's teeth. "Maybe it's because of these," I say, pointing out the jagged line on the underside of the shell. "They look like—"

"Oh yeah," says Clark. "Teeth. Never noticed that before. Clever."

I feel my cheeks go red at the compliment, but fortunately Clark's eyes are on the sand.

"Mum makes them into necklaces, bracelets and earrings," he says. "Then sells them at craft fairs and the Christmas market."

"Did she make that?" I say, pointing at the bracelet on his wrist.

Clark nods.

"Cool," I say.

"Thanks."

I spot a perfect cone-shaped shell, white and caramel like a miniature ice cream. "Any good?" I say, handing it to Clark.

"It's a painted topshell," he says. "Weird, though, isn't it?"

"The shell?"

"The whole thing," he says. "If you think about it,

these" – and he rattles his shell bag – "they're more or less the skeletons of dead sea creatures, aren't they? Sea snails and barnacles and whatnot."

"I'd never thought of it like that."

"And people keep them on shelves, make pictures out of them and turn them into jewellery. I mean, you wouldn't do that with, say, an old bird skeleton, would you? Hang it around your neck on a gold chain."

"Not unless you were a maniac," I say, and this makes Clark laugh.

He bumps me playfully with his shoulder. "You're okay," he says. "For a girl."

"Yeah, and you're not so bad either. For a boy."

I've never had boy friends. I don't mean *boyfriends*. Obviously. But friends who are boys. At school the girls hang around in one group. And the boys in another. So this is unusual for me, just walking and talking with a boy. And actually enjoying it.

But it does feel different to being with another girl. Although different how exactly, it's hard to explain. I feel happy and relaxed but also a kind of fluttery in my stomach. A bit … I don't know, 'fluttery' is the best I can do.

Clark stops and bends to pick something from the sand.

"Shell?" I ask.

"Look," he says, holding his palm out to me.

Sitting in the centre of his hand is something that looks like a blue pebble, roughly the size of my thumbnail. Clark blows the sand from it and the blue object catches the sunlight on its frosted surface. "Sea glass," he says.

"What's sea glass?"

Clark laughs. "Glass from the sea. Obviously. A bottle or dish or something that fell from a boat maybe, got smashed into tiny pieces that eventually wash up on a beach somewhere. Could have come from anywhere – America, China, India."

He runs his thumb along the edge of the small glass fragment.

"Is it sharp?"

Clark shakes his head. "The sand and water wear it smooth. The longer it's in the sea, the smoother it gets. This one must be quite old."

Clark looks out towards the sea. The breeze catches his hair and his blue eyes sparkle in the sun.

"It's pretty," I say. Clark turns to me and I drop my eyes from his face to his hand. "The sea glass, I mean."

"Here," he says, holding it out to me. "Take it."

And, again, I get that fluttery feeling in my tummy.

Maybe it's just new-friend nerves.

"Having a nice romantic walk?" says a familiar screechy voice.

Without realizing it, we have crossed the beach and come within a short distance of Hilda and her Horribles. They are leaning against a large boulder, huddled together like a trio of crabs.

Hilda giggles and blows a kiss towards us.

I feel my face go into full-on emergency blush mode.

Clark is a little cooler. "Why?" he says. "Jealous?"

"Hardly," says Hilda, but she sounds less sure of herself now. "Wouldn't waste my time on a *pov* like you."

This word – "pov" – is a word I've never heard before, but the way Hilda spits it out makes it clear it's an insult.

"What's a pov?" I say to Clark.

"It means he's poor," answers Hilda. "Lives in a crumby little house with peeling paint and a broken gate. Gets food from the food bank. Clothes from the charity shop. Look at them, they're all old and frayed with holes in them."

I look at Clark and his face gives nothing away. He stands still and tall and confident, only his hair moving in the breeze. I try not to make it obvious, but I steal a glance at his clothes, which, now that I notice, do look like they've seen better days.

"'Pov' is short for poverty," Clark says to me. "Not that Hilda knew that."

"Did," says Hilda, but her expression suggests otherwise.

Clark holds Hilda's gaze for the length of two or maybe three breaths. His silence is powerful, and you can sense Hilda's confidence fading like the tide running out to sea.

And then Clark shakes his head and huffs out a short laugh. "You know nothing, Hilda."

Like a yappy dog confronted with a bigger, stronger animal, it's clear that Hilda is outmatched. But – like little dogs will – she feels obliged to yap on anyway. Maybe to try and impress her friends.

"I know your mum cleans other people's houses," Hilda says.

Clark nods in agreement, he appears to be considering something, debating whether or not to say it. Then he nods again, as if coming to a decision. "True," he says. "And she does other people's ironing. And makes jewellery from shells. Mum will do *anything* to pay the bills. Even..." he drops his voice to a whisper, "... even breaking into houses. Didn't know *that* did you?"

Hilda shakes her head. She has lost all of her yap now.

"Do you know why burglars always carry a torch?" Clark says.

"To ... to see in the dark?"

Clark laughs. "You wouldn't make much of a burglar, would you? Torch that size would light the whole house up. The torch is in case anyone disturbs her. In case anyone tries to stop her." And with that, Clark whacks an invisible torch into his open palm. "Bang," he says, but he says it quietly. "So if I were you, *Hilda*, I'd think twice about who I call names. About who I disturb."

Her face is a mask of fear and I almost – *almost* – feel sorry for her.

"That's the thing with *povs*," Clark says. "They can get desperate. And desperate people do desperate things."

And with that, he smiles. As if we had been discussing nothing more sinister than seashells and ice cream. He turns away from the three girls and starts making his way slowly along the line that divides the beach in two. I turn and follow.

We walk in silence until we are maybe twenty paces away from the terrible trio.

"Blimey," says Clark, "that was intense."

"Is it true?" I ask him.

"What, that my mum's a burglar?"

I shake my head. "I assumed that was just you being crafty again."

Clark laughs. "You assume right. My mum wouldn't harm a fly."

"I meant … is it true about you being poor?"

"Depends what you mean by poor, I suppose. We do have to use the food bank sometimes. And I got a free spot at summer camp because Mum can't afford it."

"What about your dad?"

Clark shakes his head. "He comes and goes," he says. "And I'm not sure which is worse."

And now I feel bad for asking. "I didn't mean to—"

"It's fine." Clark bumps me again with his shoulder. "If Dad was around more I might not have come to summer camp. Might not have met you."

I'm not quite sure what to say to that, so I say nothing and walk for a while in silence. And then – perhaps because Clark has been so honest with me – I say, "My mum has depression."

"What's that?"

"It's like a sickness; it makes her sad sometimes. A lot of the time, actually. It's why we moved here."

Now I bump Clark with my shoulder. "And if not for that, I wouldn't have met you, would I?"

"Lucky us," says Clark.

"Right," I say. "Lucky us."

Clark stops walking and bends down to pick something up from the sand. He dusts it off with his fingers. "Don't see many this colour," he says, holding out his palm to show me a red, diamond-shaped piece of sea glass.

"Like a ruby," I say.

"Exactly," says Clark. "Who needs money when you have rubies?" And he passes the piece of glass to me. "For your collection."

And as I take the glass, my tummy flutters.

Fort #47

I have decided to make a sea-glass necklace for Mum's birthday. Clark said he would help me, and Jody has a whole bunch of necklace-making stuff at Camp Sunshine. I have three pieces of sea glass now. Two that Clark found and a white piece nestled among the seaweed that caught my eye. Not enough for a necklace yet, but Mum's birthday is not for another three weeks. I still have time.

I've been thinking about sea glass. About the way it started as one thing – a bottle, a plate, a glass – then became something new. Like a necklace.

I've been thinking about how before sea glass can become something beautiful, like a necklace, it has to first be broken – smashed against the rocks of the ocean bed.

And I've been thinking too, about the way those broken pieces are transformed by the patient work of fine sand and salty seawater, which slowly, steadily, wear away the jagged edges, making them clean and smooth.

And, of course, time. How all of this – the breaking, the smoothing, the becoming something new – how all of it takes time.

And I've been thinking that maybe sometimes it's like that for people too. They start out as perfect glasses, mirrors, cups, bottles. But something – it doesn't matter what – damages and cracks and hurts them.

Like what happened to my mum.

And maybe we – me and Dad – maybe we are the sand and the seawater. Maybe it is our job to gently, patiently smooth away the sharpness and jaggedness and make something new. We just need to give it time.

12
A Skye Full of Stars

As well as plastic pollution, big cities like London have light pollution. This means the sky is so full of light – from all the millions of houses and cars and towers – that you can't see the stars at night. It's better in Cliffside Village. At night-time here the sky is full of stars, like a fine dust on a black sheet. But even that's nothing compared to the island where my grandparents come from. Where they come from, the sky feels like it's bursting with stars, all crammed together and shining bright as Christmas lights.

That, Granddad says, is why it is called the Isle of Skye.

He tells me this every time we visit. I think maybe because he has the dementia and can't remember that he's told me before. But I like the way he talks about the stars in the Skye sky – as if he's proud of them, almost as if he placed them there himself.

In fact, I like the way Granddad talks about

anything. He has a deep Scottish accent and uses lots of words I don't hear from anyone else.

When we video called them tonight, he blew me a kiss through the computer screen and said in his Scottish accent, "Ach, an how's ma bonnie wee grandbairn?"

Which means, *how's my beautiful little grandchild.*

And I told him, "Guid."

Which means *good.*

Because Gran and Granddad haven't seen our new house, we walked from room to room with the computer, showing them our new home and even outside in the garden. Granddad was confused at first – he'd forgotten that we've moved house – but he seems to have the hang of it now.

"So much green!" Gran says, talking about the fields and trees that stretch out towards the sea. "It must remind you of home."

"A little," says Mum.

Mum grew up in Skye, but she doesn't speak like Gran and Granddad do. Maybe because she hasn't lived there for so long. And it's funny, I think, how where we live changes us. Like Mum leaving her accent behind in Scotland. And – if Dad's right about Cliffside Cove – leaving her depression behind in London.

"How are the stars there?" Granddad asks.

"They're beautiful, Dad," says Mum.

Granddad makes a little harrumphing noise at this, as if he isn't convinced.

"But not as beautiful as those at home," Mum adds, and this seems to satisfy Granddad.

"Well, we've the clearest sky y'll ever see," he says. "And stars to make your eyes water. That's why it's called the Isle of Skye, you know?"

On the computer screen Gran grins and rolls her eyes.

"Have you taken a dip in the sea yet?" she says.

Mum hasn't even been to the cove yet, but she doesn't say this to her mum. She just says that she hasn't done any swimming.

"And what about you, Phyllis?" Granddad asks.

"No swimming," I say, "but the cove is amazing. I found sea glass. There used to be pirates here, so maybe it's from a pirate ship."

"Pirates?" says Gran. "Well you just be careful, okay?"

"Oh, they're not here now," I tell her, and Gran seems to find this very funny.

"Well," says Gran, "we have a bit of news. Bit of a surprise, actually."

"Oh?" says Mum. "Nothing…" She pulls a face.

"Oh nothing bad, love. It's rather exciting, really."

"What is it?" Dad asks.

"Someone," Gran says, "is having a baby. Well, several babies."

"Are you pregnant, Gran?" I ask, and Granddad, who has just taken a sip of his drink, suddenly turns red as if he is choking. He turns his head away from the computer just before he coughs up a mouthful of coffee, which goes spraying out to the side.

"What was all that about?" Gran says to him.

"You're pregnant?" he says.

"I'm seventy-three, you great fool."

Granddad looks at Gran as if this is new information to him. "Really?"

Mum bursts out laughing at this, then Dad joins in too.

"Yes," says Gran. "Really."

"So who's up the duff?" Granddad says.

"Pregnant," says Mum.

Gran bends down so that I can't see her properly. I hear her grunt, and when she comes back into the picture, she's holding a small brown and white dog.

"Josie!" says Mum. "Hello, girl."

"Full of puppies," says Gran.

"Puppies!" I say, and my voice is all high and excited. "When are they coming?"

"Hard to say," Gran says. "Four weeks, perhaps. Maybe five."

"How many?"

"Too early to tell, sweetheart. But it'll be a few, that's for sure."

"Will you keep them all?"

"Will we heck," says Granddad. "Enough animals already."

Gran gives him a sideways look. "We'll see," she says. "We might keep one. Or two."

"One," says Granddad.

And Gran smiles like she's just won something.

"Maybe you could come and visit," Gran says. "I mean," she hesitates, "if you feel up to it, love."

Mum sighs gently beside me. "I'd love to," she says, "when things are…"

"When things are more settled," Dad says, and he reaches across to hold Mum's hand.

"Of course," says Gran. And she smiles into the computer, but her smile looks like it's an effort, like Mum's does when it won't go all the way to her eyes. "Of course."

13

A Coincidence

There are two different roads that lead from Camp Sunshine to our new house, and today I took the road that runs past Ocean Breeze old folks' home. I had an idea that maybe I would stop in and say hello to Mr Djinn, but when I got there, he was sitting in a wheelchair in the gardens and staring out towards the sea with a faraway look in his eyes.

I stood there for a few seconds not knowing quite what to say, then Mr Djinn turned his eyes towards me and said – as if we had been talking for the past ten minutes – "Let's go inside where it's cooler."

And so we did.

We're playing cribbage (Mr Djinn was right, it really is a very good game), and talking at the same time. Well, it's mostly me talking while Mr Djinn listens about how we searched for, and eventually found, Mum's copy of *1001 Nights*. And how it has exactly the same cover as his copy of the same book.

"What a coincidence," he says with a smile.

"I know!" And as I say it, I glance down at the table and notice that Mr Djinn's copy is no longer there.

"Wait, what happened to your book?" I ask him.

"Who knows?" he says. "Perhaps I misplaced it. That happens a lot."

"Don't you think that's strange?" I say. "That Mum found her copy of the book at the same time you lost yours?"

Mr Djinn shrugs, as if, no, he doesn't find this massive coincidence in the least bit strange. He plays a card then looks at me, waiting for me to play mine.

I turn my attention to my cards and lay one on the table.

"Two points," says Mr Djinn. "You're learning."

In cribbage, you play as many hands as it takes for someone to score 121 points. Right now, Mr Djinn has 82 points against my 52. I think I know who's going to win.

"Mum said it's not suitable for little girls," I say.

"Cribbage?"

"The book. *1001 Nights*."

Mr Djinn plays his last card, bringing this particular hand to an end. "Your mother is very wise," he says. "There is much wickedness in those stories."

"She said I can read it when I'm fifteen."

"The time will pass quickly," says Mr Djinn. Then he adds up our scores, shuffles the cards and deals a new hand.

"We're reading *Treasure Island* now," I say.

"Ah, pirates!"

"You've read it?"

Mr Djinn nods. "And very true to life it is too. Once upon a time, I was captured by pirates."

He inspects the cards in his hand and lays one on the table between us.

"Wait," I say. "Did you just say *pirates*?"

14

The Merchant and the Pirate

Mr Djinn looks me in the eye and smiles.

"I have had many masters in my long life. I have been in the service of commoners and royalty, soldiers and artists, the kind, the cruel, the wise and the foolish. One such master was a seafaring merchant; a singularly greedy man who sailed from country to country trading silks and spices and other extravagant items. When I offered him three wishes, can you guess the first thing he requested?"

"More wishes?"

Mr Djinn claps his hands. "You have inherited your mother's wisdom, I see. Yes, more wishes. But wishes do not work that way," he says. "Otherwise, what would be the point of offering three wishes in the first place?"

"No point at all."

"Correct," says Mr Djinn. "So instead of wishes, the merchant wished for gold. One hundred chests of it.

Enough to last many lifetimes, but not so much that he could not carry it with him wherever he went."

"How do you carry one hundred chests of gold?"

"With a fleet of one hundred ships," says Mr Djinn. "Which is what the merchant wished for next."

"What was his third wish?"

"The third wish troubled the merchant greatly. He knew it would be his last and could not decide how to use it. He worried about the question day and night, and sought the advice of wise men and women from all corners of the earth. And during this time – this voyage of many years – I remained in a dark glass bottle which the merchant kept locked in a safe in his cabin."

"It must have been boring," I say. "Being locked in a bottle all that time."

"I slept," says Mr Djinn. "And a most pleasant slumber it was too. Until, after several years, I was rudely awakened by the sound of canon fire and screaming."

"Pirates?" I guess.

"Exactly, child. News of the merchant and his genie had reached many ears. One of which bore a gold earring and belonged to none other than Blackbeard – the most fearsome pirate ever to raise a sail. It was not difficult for Blackbeard to locate the merchant – a fleet of one hundred ships is, after all, a conspicuous thing.

"And so I awoke to the sound of men screaming and muskets firing. The pirates boarded the merchant's ship and set about dispatching his crew."

"Dispatching?"

"Bashing them on the head, slashing at them with swords, tossing them into the waves. And now the merchant knew exactly how he must use his final wish."

"To dispatch Blackbeard?"

"Exactly so. He ran to fetch me from his cabin, but because he had left me alone for so long, the safe door had rusted tight shut. The merchant was still struggling with the key when Blackbeard kicked in his door. To cut a long story short, the merchant was thrown overboard, the safe was unlocked and I found myself with a new master."

"He sounds dreadful."

Mr Djinn smiles as if at a fond memory. "He was a scoundrel, to be sure. But it is not a genie's place to judge. Besides, Blackbeard was good company and he treated me well."

All the while, we have been playing cribbage and, once again, the six cards are laid and we add up our scores. Mr Djinn is on 114 now, while I am only on 74.

"You are doing well," he says. "I have been playing for a very, *very* long time, remember."

"What did Blackbeard wish for?" I ask.

Mr Djinn shuffles and deals the cards before answering. "He wished for nothing."

"Nothing? Nothing at all?"

"Blackbeard was an unusually clever fellow and he immediately understood what the merchant had not. That wishes must run out. And when they do, the wisher may have gold and palaces and elephants, but he will be – like he was before – without wishes. Without magic."

"So Blackbeard wished for nothing?"

"There is an expression," Mr Djinn says. "Perhaps you have heard it? *Be careful what you wish for.*"

"Maybe," I say. "I'm not sure."

He smiles and says, "It means that what you think you want, doesn't always turn out the way you think it will. People, for example, wish for money, thinking it will make them happy. But when you have money, you will find no shortage of people who want to take it from you. And this makes no one happy. The same is true of many things that people wish for – power, knowledge, even love. And Blackbeard understood this."

"About wishes?"

"About life. He possessed all he needed – ships, power, more gold than he could ever spend. The only danger, of course, was being apprehended by the authorities or attacked by other pirates. But now he had a genie in his crew, and word of this travelled far and fast. Blackbeard was fearsome enough, but with a genie at his side, no one would ever dare attack him."

"Blackbeard attacked the merchant," I say. "And he had a genie."

"True, child. But Blackbeard was – as I believe I have explained – a rare and crafty fellow. And as such, he kept me not for wishes, but as a symbol. The way ancient tribes would wear animal bones around their necks to inspire fear in their enemies."

Mr Djinn places a card on the table. "Two points."

I lay one of my own. No points.

"How did you escape?" I ask. "From Blackbeard?"

"We spent a lot of time on deck, talking, smoking pipes and playing cards. And at night he would return me to my bottle, which he wore on a chain around his neck, tucked under his jacket where no one could steal it."

"So what did you do?"

"Me? Nothing. It was a fish pie that did it."

"Pie?"

"It may have been tuna, but I don't recall. What I do remember, is that not long after it went down, it came straight back up. Perhaps the fish was bad, maybe it was not cooked properly, but within an hour of it being served, all the crew were leaning over the taffrail and returning their suppers to the ocean."

"They were being sick?"

Mr Djinn nods. "Most violently. Blackbeard included. And, during his exertions, the bottle slipped from his jacket and the chain slipped from around his neck. The bottle tumbled into the ocean. Your turn," he says, pointing to my cards.

I play an ace of clubs, and Mr Djinn nods. "Two points, very good."

"What happened then?" I ask.

"The bottle settled gently on the ocean bed, and there it would have remained – with me inside – for many years, until, perhaps, the end of time. But I was fortunate. Did you know there are storms beneath the sea?"

I shake my head.

"Well, thank goodness there are," he says. "And in one such storm, my bottle was tossed about like a pea in a pot. A stone struck the bottle knocking a neat hole in the side. And I was – as I am now – free."

Mr Djinn lays an ace of diamonds on top of my ace of clubs. "Six points," he says, "and the game. But you came closer this time."

15

Young Knees
and Plenty of Energy

Mr Djinn gathers up the cards and returns them to the deck. He taps this firmly against the table – first along one edge, then the other – making the stack neat and square.

"Now, Phyllis, it is your turn."

"To shuffle?"

"To tell me something. I told you about Blackbeard. Now you tell something to me."

"Tell you what?"

"Something wonderful."

"I'm only eleven."

Mr Djinn smiles. "Then tell me, Phyllis, what is wonderful to an eleven-year-old girl?"

"Oh, I know!"

"Yes?"

"My grandparents are having puppies," I say. "Well, Josie, their dog is. They already have four dogs, so they'll have absolutely loads when the puppies come."

Mr Djinn smiles at this and nods, almost as if the news were expected.

"A dog is a wonderful thing," he says, again looking deep, deep into my eyes. "You would like one of your own, I think?"

I nod, and when I do I feel a lump in my throat, as if I might cry. Because, yes, I would *love* a puppy, I would walk it and cuddle it and look after it and brush its fur, but this is something I can't have. My mind begins to form the words, *I wish I had a puppy*, but...

Mr Djinn is still watching me, closely but also gently, and I remember his words from when he was telling me about Blackbeard: *be careful what you wish for.* And now, with his eyes firmly on mine, I feel that those words are directed at me. And so I push the unmade wish to the back of my mind. For now, at least.

Mr Djinn blinks, and returns his attention to the cards in his hand.

"They will be very busy, I think."

"Who?"

"Your grandparents. There will be a lot of dogs to walk, which is not so easy for older folks with creaky knees and so on. They will need help, I think. Someone with young knees and plenty of energy."

"Yes," I say, "I suppose they will."

"I hope they find someone suitable," says Mr Djinn. "Suitable people can be hard to find."

The sound of rattling cups and saucers draws our attention. It is one of the carers pushing the tea trolley.

"I should probably go," I say.

"Of course," says Mr Djinn. With some effort, he turns around and unhooks an umbrella from the back of his chair. It is not at all the sort of umbrella I would expect an old man to own – pink, with white polka dots and a red trim. It's so bright, I wonder how I hadn't noticed it earlier. Maybe because I was so engrossed in the cards and in his story.

"Here," he says, holding the umbrella out to me.

"It's not raining," I tell him.

"Oh," he says. But the way he says it sounds like a question, *oh?*

And then, beyond the windows, the sky darkens and thunder cracks across the sky.

I take the umbrella.

16

Someone
– in Other Words –
Like Me

I should be sleeping, but the storm is still howling outside.

One of my window panes is loose and it rattles in the frame. Rain taps against the glass like bony fingers. The wind is made of many different sounds as it swoops through trees and around the roof; it moans and wails and it sounds like the voices of ghosts. I hear a bell ringing in the direction of the sea, a faint and echoing clang, but maybe – with my mind full of pirate stories – this is nothing more than my imagination.

Mum read *Treasure Island* again tonight, and – it's too early to be certain – it might be my new favourite book. Dad says Long John Silver from the book wasn't a real pirate, but he said Blackbeard was. So there was at least some truth in Mr Djinn's tale of the Merchant and the Pirate.

In my room I have a clock shaped like a puppy's face and the eyes shift left and right with each tick of the second hand. In the daytime, it's funny. But now, with the ghosts of pirates tapping on my window pane, the puppy's glow-in-the-dark eyes look terrified as it ticks towards two o'clock in the morning.

But I'm okay. I like the sounds and the drama and the make-believe world outside. Because that's all it is. Make believe. There are no pirate ghosts.

There are no genies.

That's what I keep telling myself.

Except, myself keeps answering back, in a quiet and cautious voice…

Are you sure?

But more than pirates and genies, what I'm thinking about as I lie here in the dark is puppies. And what Mr Djinn said about my grandparents needing someone suitable to help them walk their dogs. I suppose a suitable person would be someone who loved dogs. Like I do. Except of course, I am hundreds of miles away.

I feel an idea pushing at the front of my brain, like a chick inside an egg, gently tapping its beak against the shell as it attempts to break through.

And then it comes: there are lots of people with dogs in *my* corner of the country. On my edge of England, up against the sea. And maybe some of those people need someone suitable to walk *their* dogs.

Someone – in other words – like me.

I turn on my reading light and quietly slip out of bed.

I find paper and coloured pencils, and – leaning on my big *Dog Encyclopaedia* – I start work on a leaflet. The first three words are easy, and I write them in fat red capitals: FREE DOG WALKING.

17
Going Away

"Did anyone call yet?" Clark asks.

After I finished creating the leaflets offering my services as a free dog-walker, I crawled back into bed and fell into a deep sleep, dreaming a mad dream featuring genies, dogs and pirates. The next day, Dad took my leaflet into work, scanned it into his computer and printed off a bunch of copies, which the two of us posted through letterboxes that same evening. Dad said he was proud of me for showing initiative instead of just sitting around and hoping things will happen.

Except nothing has happened.

I shake my head, "Not yet."

"Well," says Clark, "it's only been one day. Someone's bound to call."

I'm teaching him to play cribbage under the shade of the palm tree at Camp Sunshine. Hilda has been relatively quiet, but twice when I've walked past her I have heard her making kissing sounds behind my back. I assume this is meant to suggest that Clark and I are boyfriend and girlfriend, even though the idea is totally ridiculous.

"Your hair's growing," Clark says now.

"Hair tends to do that," I tell him.

"Another couple of months and I could almost do something with it," he says. "It'd look good with a French plait."

And my stupid face goes and blushes again. It's very annoying.

Clark looks like he's about to say something, probably about my face being as red as a tomato, but he appears to change his mind and drops his eyes to his cards. "It's a good game," he says.

"That man at the old folks' home taught me."

Clark plays a king and scores two points. "The one with the earring? He looks cool," Clark says.

"He is."

It's tempting to tell Clark all about Mr Djinn. But in the same way that I hesitated to tell my parents about his mad ideas, I hesitate to tell Clark. Some things, I think, are best kept to yourself.

I pick up the cards, shuffle them and deal a new hand of six cards to each of us.

"How many leaflets did you post?" Clark asks.

"Sixteen," I tell him. "But I'm not even sure all of them have dogs."

"Imagine if they all did," he says. "And they all called and asked you to walk their dogs."

"Maybe you could help me," I say, the words coming out of my mouth before I have a chance to think about them.

"Sure," Clark says. "Except..."

"Except what?"

Clark pulls a face as if he's about to tell me bad news. And then he does just that.

"I'm going away," he says.

"What? What do you mean?"

"Holiday." He says the word the way you would expect him to say "dentist". As if, rather than something fun, a holiday were something to be dreaded.

"Oh," I say, feeling disappointed and relieved at the same time. Disappointed that he's going away; relieved that it's only for a holiday and not for ever. "Where are you going?"

"Edinburgh. We're staying with my auntie."

"My grandparents live on an island at the top of Scotland," I tell him.

"Ha," says Clark. "I wonder if I'll see them. Scotland's tiny."

"Maybe," I say. Then, "I suppose it'll be nice to spend some time with your mum and dad."

"It's just me and Mum. She wants ... she wants some time away from Dad." Clark inspects his cards and after some thought lays one down. "I don't know why they don't just get divorced," he says.

"I'm sorry. It must be..." and I realize that I have absolutely no idea what it must be like.

Clark nods. Perhaps he can't figure out what it's like either.

"How long are you going away for?"

Clark shrugs. "A week. Maybe two."

"Two weeks! When are you going?"

He smiles apologetically. "Tonight."

My stomach clenches and I feel as if something important has been snatched from my hands. "Tonight?"

Clark nods slowly.

"You're abandoning me," I say, trying to make a joke out of the situation. "Leaving me to the mercy of Hilda and the Horribles."

"You can handle them," Clark says.

"Well, I'll have to, won't I?"

And although I said it as a joke, the idea of dealing with Hilda on my own is a scary one. It's easy for Clark to say I can handle her – he's braver than me, and I'm pretty sure Hilda can sense that. I suppose I'll just have to pretend. The way you have to pretend you're not scared of a growly dog. Even if you are.

Clark twists the seashell bracelet around his wrist, and I'm reminded of Mr Djinn saying that ancient tribes used to wear animal bones to scare their enemies. And how Clark said that seashells are basically the old bones of sea creatures.

"Could I..." I point at Clark's bracelet, "...could I borrow that, do you think? While you're away?"

Clark smiles. "Sure," he says, removing the bracelet and passing it to me. Where the bracelet used to lie, there is a bright white gap in his suntan.

"Thank you," I say, slipping the bracelet onto my wrist.

To inspire fear in my enemies, I think.

And then I lay a card on top of Clark's. "Two points."

18

A Short Phone Call

Walking home I have the feeling that I have left something important behind at Camp Sunshine. And then I realize that thing is Clark. At the end of the day, we stood outside and said goodbye, not quite knowing how to do such a simple thing.

I felt that we should hug, and if Clark had been a girl, that's exactly what I would have done. But other people were hanging around, including Hilda and her Horribles. So we just said, "See you." And Clark rode one way on his bike while I went the other way on foot.

At the bench beneath the lost dog poster, I stop to sit and think and rest my feet.

The poster is more ragged than ever – the paper is rippled and the ink has run from all the rain we've been having. You can't read the phone number any more, and the way the ink has run, it almost looks as if Tim – the lost dog – is crying. And I think *yes, Tim, I know how you feel*.

Before I've even thought about what I'm doing, I take my phone out of my bag and call Tim's owner. After only three rings, a lady's voice answers. "Hello? Who is this please?" She sounds like she might be a similar age to my granny.

"I'm Phyllis," I say, thinking that if I introduce myself as Phyll over the phone, this lady might mistake me for a boy.

"Oh," says the lady. "And what can I do for you, Phyllis?"

"It's about your lost dog poster."

The lady is suddenly excited. "Have you found him? Have you found my Timmy?"

"Oh, no," I say, realizing only now what a terrible idea this was. "No, I'm sorry, I … I just saw the poster and—"

"You haven't found him?" the woman says, and her voice has gone all wobbly.

"I'm sorry, no. But the poster is all wet and tatty and the number – the ink got wet, you see, and if anyone does find Tim, they won't be able to read your number. So I thought maybe you might want to put a new one up."

"Oh," says the lady, "I see. I … but how did you know the number?"

I explain how I had saved the number in case I ever found him.

"How thoughtful of you," says the lady. "How very, very thoughtful."

"I'm sure he'll turn up," I say.

The lady sniffs. It sounds like she is crying, and it's a moment before she speaks again. "Oh, I wish he would, Phyllis. I really wish he would."

"Yes," I say, "I really wish he would too."

Maybe the sun passes behind a cloud, because I all of a sudden shiver, as if cold fingers have walked up the length of my back. But when I glance up to the sky, it is a perfect and cloudless blue and the sun is warm against my face.

Fort #48

A lost dog poster, I think, is one of the saddest things in the world. It's like a very short story with a beginning and a disaster but no happy ending. Or none that you know of.

You see the picture of the little dog, taken at a time when everything was okay. When the dog had no idea that there was even such a thing as "lost". Because, let's be honest, dogs aren't too smart.

And because this dog is daft, it probably can't imagine how its situation will end. It doesn't know anyone is looking for it. It doesn't know its face is on a lamppost. This dog is just lost and alone, and that — as far as it understands — is the way the world is now.

I think about Tim the lost dog, cold and wet and hungry probably. Confused and frightened and alone.

And this thought makes me want to cry. Because, in a way, I know how he must feel. I'm far from the place I still think of as home, far from my friends and the places I know. Even Clark is going away.

And yes, Tim, I know how you feel. I feel lost and lonely too.

But no one has pinned my face to a lamppost. There is no poster that says "LOST GIRL". There is no number to call.

So it's down to me. I'll have to find my own happy ending.

I just need to figure out where to look.

19
Just Coffee

"This is very good coffee," Mr Djinn says, after I pour him a cup from the thermos flask. "And you made this yourself?"

"This morning," I tell him.

Dad had to leave early for a meeting, so I ate breakfast alone, sitting outside in the morning sunshine, then pottered around, cleaning the kitchen and tidying up the TV room. In the library room, the books remain half unpacked, arranged in unsteady heaps and scattered in piles. They seem sad and forgotten, so I closed the door, hiding them from sight. Then, before leaving for camp, I filled a thermos flask all the way to the top with fresh, hot coffee.

"Ha! And still warm," says Mr Djinn. "You know, Phyllis, I think you have something of the genie in you."

"It's just coffee," I say, trying to sound modest.

"Not *just* coffee," Mr Djinn says, wagging a knobbly finger at me. "A wish, *my wish*, for a good cup of java.

Which is what this" – he pauses to smell the aroma of the coffee, just like Dad does – "most certainly is. Thank you, child, you are very kind."

I blush and mutter something about Mr Djinn being welcome.

Mr Djinn puts a hand to his mouth and begins coughing. He coughs so much that his eyes water and red colour rises behind his deep brown skin. When the coughing passes, he reaches for a glass of water, but his hands are trembling slightly, and when he lifts the glass, a few drops spill down the front of his shirt.

"Are you okay?" I ask.

"In a manner of speaking. My body misbehaves, this cough, these hands. They give me enough tablets to fill a bottle every day, but I don't think they do what they're meant to do. But this is the way of things, and – the short answer to your question – yes, I am fine."

He doesn't look fine. He looks like he has aged many years in the few days since I last saw him. His skin looks more lined, and it doesn't glow like it once did. His eyes, even his voice, seem very tired today.

"Are you still enjoying *Treasure Island*?" he asks.

I tell him that I am, but a more accurate answer would be I *was*.

The book sits on the windowsill in my room,

splayed open at the start of chapter five which is where we got to before the clouds drifted in again. Mum has been mostly in bed for the last few days, and although Dad said he would read to me, I want to wait until the clouds pass and we can continue reading as a family.

Mr Djinn looks at me, like he is reading my expression, or maybe even my thoughts. He smiles gently and pats my hand, as if in that touch he is saying, *It will be okay, Phyllis. Everything will be okay.*

He turns my hand over in his and his eyes go to the not-very-good sea-glass bracelet on my wrist.

"You made this?"

I nod. "At camp today."

"It's very lovely," Mr Djinn says. Which is kind of him, because it's actually a complete mess.

"It's practice," I say. "For when I make one for my mum's birthday."

"I think she will like that, my little genie." And he winks. "I think she will love it."

"It's only sea glass."

Mr Djinn nods. "And diamonds are only rocks, gold is only metal. The material does not matter. I have placed many gems and much money in the hands of men and women, do you think it made them happy?"

"Yes?"

Mr Djinn laughs. "Yes, it almost always did. But wealth brings its own problems and the happiness did not always last. Neither, for that matter, did the money."

"Were you rich?" I ask.

And I realize that I am asking the question as if Mr Djinn has, as he claims, placed many gems in the hands of men and women. As if he were, after all, a genie. Not that I necessarily believe he is, rather that if he is going to make the claim, I might as well go along with it and enjoy the game of pretend.

"I cannot grant my own wishes," he says. "I cannot create money for myself. But yes, I have been rich."

"How?"

"Like anyone else," he says. "I worked."

"What as?"

"Ah, many, many things. You'd be surprised how many jobs involve the granting – in one way or another – of wishes. I have worked in banks and movie studios and advertising agencies. I have travelled with rock-and-roll bands and orchestras. I have served ale from behind a bar, I have cooked for kings. I have seen babies enter the world, and held the hands of the sick as they left it behind. I have advised wise men and cautioned fools. I once worked on a vineyard, but only because I like good wine. And, through it all, Phyllis,

I learned to read men's minds from the lines in their brow, to understand women's wishes from the shape of their smile. And, yes, I accumulated a great deal of money."

"Are you...?"

"Am I rich now?" Mr Djinn laughs. "No. The money has been spent wisely, squandered joyously and given to those who needed it more than me. And I am glad to be rid of it, Phyllis."

"Why would you be glad to be poor?"

"I never said I was poor. I said I had no money. And much better for me that way. Money draws attention, and the very last thing I want is attention."

"Why not?"

"In case anyone realized I was a genie. Because if that happens" – he clicks his fingers – "the next thing you know you're trapped in a lamp for two thousand years. Better to be free," he says. "That is what it means to be rich – to be master of your own destiny rather than the servant of another. And so I draw no attention, I keep my secrets, I lie low."

"But you told *me*. You told *me* you're a genie."

"I did, child, but I have a feeling I can trust you. Besides, I am old now. Who would possibly believe I am a genie?"

He looks at me carefully now, as if he expects me to comment. Perhaps he hopes I will tell him that I believe. The silence is a little awkward.

"Well, little genie," Mr Djinn says, smiling. "I believe in *you*."

He reaches for his coffee, takes a sip and closes his eyes in pleasure.

"Yes," he says. "I believe in you."

20

Dog

Maybe this is what it's like being a millionaire. Floating on my back in my swimming pool, the sun warm and orange through my closed eyelids, the breeze on my face and the sound of gulls overhead.

Except my swimming pool is really a paddling pool. But as paddling pools go, it's a big one. Big enough for me to float in a star shape and not touch the round wall with either fingers or toes. The wall is made of multi-coloured bands so that if I open my eyes underwater, it's like being inside a rainbow.

When I got home from the old folks' home, it was all inflated and filled – a surprise present from Dad who finished work early and set it up in the front garden. With my head underwater, I can hear him working nearby, sawing planks of wood for his mysterious project. From underwater, the saw sounds like a snoring sea monster. I have to be quiet to avoid waking it, so I swim slowly underwater, and when I come up for air,

I come up quietly. You have to be careful around sea monsters.

"Thought you'd drowned," Dad says, as my head peeps over the edge of my awesome pool.

Dad has a workbench in the garden and stacks of wood that he is carefully measuring, marking with a pencil and cutting to length.

"Tell me," I say.

Dad shakes his head. "Secret."

"I won't tell."

"I know. But I think you'll like the surprise."

"Bah," I say, and I sink again under the rainbow water and imagine I am looking for pirate treasure. Or a dropped genie bottle.

Dad's making a present for Mum's birthday. He says he was inspired by me making her a sea-glass necklace. That he thought he would make something too. I can only imagine it's a box of some kind; maybe a trunk for keeping things in. Or a chest. Or maybe a bench, or one of those swing-seats some people have in their garden.

Whatever it is, Dad isn't telling.

I'm turning an underwater somersault when I hear a strange warbling sound. There's something familiar about the noise and I close my eyes as I try to identify it. And then Dad calls my name. He shouts, "Phone!"

I pop my head above the water and hear it now – my phone, ringing in the kitchen.

My heart jumps – no one has my phone number except Mum and Dad, so this could mean only one thing.

"A dog!" I say. "It has to be about a dog."

Dad puts down his saw and jogs into the house while I scramble out of the pool. I get to the kitchen just as Dad is answering the call. My hands are wet so he holds the phone to my ear.

"Hello," I say, trying to sound friendly and reliable. Like the kind of girl you would trust with your dog.

"You the girl walkin' dogs?" says a gruff voice. He asks the question as if he's accusing me of doing something wrong. As if he's saying, *Are you the girl who smashed my windows?*

"Yes," I say, a little fearfully.

"An' it's free? Cos if you want payin', I ain't payin'."

"It's free," I say. "I'd just like to walk a d—"

"Fifteen minutes," the man says.

"Excuse me?"

He sighs down the phone. "You can walk him in fifteen minutes."

Dad has his ear close to mine, so he can hear the conversation too.

I look at him and mouth the words, "*Can we?*"

Dad points to the oven where our lasagne is cooking. He rubs his tummy as if he is starving and mouths the words: *In an hour?*

"Well?" says the man impatiently.

"We were just about to have supper," I say. "Perhap—"

"That's your business," he says, interrupting. "I've my own things to do. Fifteen minutes or not at all. All the same to me."

I look again at Dad and Dad nods. *Okay.*

"Yes," I say, and I can hardly contain my excitement. "Yes!"

The dog is called Dog.

He is the same brown colour as a cup of coffee, except his fur is scruffy and tangled and a little bit stinky. He is coffee-coloured all over except for a lighter patch on the side of his leg that is as big as a digestive biscuit and more or less the same colour. I wonder why they didn't call him Spot, or Patch.

"Right," the man said when we came to the door. Not "hello" or "nice to meet you" or "thank you for walking my dog". Just "Right", and he walked around the side of the house to a gate leading to his back garden.

The man opened the gate and a scruffy dog sprang up and started barking.

"Dog!" the man said in a loud voice that was the next best thing to shouting. "Stay!"

As the man shuffled towards the dog, the animal lowered its snout to the ground but never took its eyes from the man. As if it were afraid of him. As the dog dipped its nose, I saw that it was chained to a pole in the centre of the garden. And around the pole, worn into the grass, was a muddy circular track where the dog had obviously run round and round in circles at the end of his not-very-long chain.

The man unlocked the chain, attached a lead to Dog's collar and led him out of the garden.

"Here," he said, handing the tatty lead to me. I took the lead and Dog shot off up the driveway so fast he nearly pulled my arm off. The man gave a mean laugh.

"I'm Derek," Dad said, holding out his hand.

The man looked at Dad's hand but didn't go to shake it. He said, "Be back in hour," and went to close the door.

"What's his name?" I asked quickly.

"Dog," the man said.

"Yes," I answered.

The man looked at me like I was stupid. "Yes?

Whaddya mean 'yes'?"

"She means," Dad said, and his voice sounded firm, like he didn't very much care for this man. "What's the dog called? What's its name?"

"Dog's called Dog," the man said and he closed the door.

Dog's back is as high as my legs, but he's skinny despite being so tall. And strong, despite being so skinny. I have two hands on the lead and it still feels like at any moment he might run off and drag me along helplessly behind him.

"Want me to take the lead?" Dad asks.

"No way," I tell him. "No way. We're fine, aren't we, Dog?"

Dog. I don't know if his name is funny or just lazy. Imagine if your name was Boy, or Girl, or Human – it would feel pretty weird. Also, any time anyone says the word "dog", Dog probably thinks they're talking to him. And wondering how on Earth they know his name.

If I was going to give him a name it would be Dunk, like you do with biscuits in coffee.

I pat Dog on his biscuit-coloured patch. "It's a funny name, isn't it, Dog?"

Dog's ears twitch and he does a short bark that you could almost imagine sounds like a husky "Yes".

"Maybe he thinks Phyllis is a funny name too," Dad says.

"Well, you picked it."

We have no plan as we walk, we simply follow Dog, the lead pulled out tight and my arms at full stretch as I struggle to hold onto him.

Now that I think of it, Dog is walking us instead of the other way around. He changes direction often, dragging us up side streets, down footpaths and across fields.

After maybe fifteen minutes, Dog has brought us to the beach and he tugs even harder on the lead as we make our way down the steep steps.

"He wants to go off the lead," Dad says.

"Should we let him?"

Dad pulls a face like he's not sure. "I'd hate to lose him. His owner doesn't seem particularly understanding."

"He wasn't very friendly."

"You can say that again," Dad says. And I can never resist when Dad says this, so of course, I say it again, and when we laugh, Dog starts barking like he is laughing too.

"I think it'll be fine down here," Dad says. "It's not

like he can run into the road or anything. And that lead looks like it's going to snap. Let's do it."

We unclip the lead and Dog is off and running like escaped lightning, bounding in sharp and rapid zigzags as if he doesn't know quite what to do with his freedom. His paws kick up clouds of sand as he darts and turns and twists, chasing his tail, chasing shadows, chasing nothing but fresh air. He bounds towards the shore and barks at the waves, his tail wagging in wide swishes from left to right.

Dad and I start to follow, but because he changes direction so often, we soon give up on this and instead find a big rock to sit on and watch. Dad has picked up a stick and he uses it to draw a cartoon dog in the sand. He passes the stick to me and I copy his sketch so that the cartoon dog now has a friend.

"Remember when Mum buried me?" I say.

Dad laughs.

We were on another beach, but I don't remember where. Cornwall, maybe. And Mum started dropping handfuls of warm sand onto my feet. Just small handfuls at first, then when my feet were completely covered she moved onto my legs and tummy and chest, slowly covering me until only my head was left out.

"The treasure chest," Dad says.

After I was covered, Mum started shaping the sand, piling up the sides and adding more so that it felt like a warm heavy blanket on my chest and tummy. Heaping it on and sculpting it until she had made not a sandcastle, but a sand treasure chest, like the ones you see in pirate films.

"There," she said. "Now you're treasure."

And if I close my eyes, I can still feel the weight of sand on my tummy. I can still see Mum's easy smile as she carefully decorated the trunk with rows of seashells.

The sound of Dog barking pulls me out of the memory and back to this beach and this moment. Dog comes running towards us, but at the last moment he curves off, loops around us and heads back to the waves. His head bobs up and down as he runs and it's so silly and lovely and happy that it just makes me smile.

"I wonder if he'll tire out," I say.

Dad laughs. "I wouldn't bet on it."

Dog is again barking at the waves, as if warning them against coming any further.

"Just as long as he doesn't run into the sea," Dad says.

Then, of course, Dog does exactly that.

"Oh well," says Dad. "He looked like he needed a good bath."

Dog leaps over one incoming wave and lands with a splash and a bark of what sounds to me like pure delight. Another wave rolls in and Dog leaps this one too. Without saying anything, Dad and I get up from our rock and walk towards the shoreline where the silly dog is barking and wagging and playing his new game. Something about it makes me want to play too, and Dad must feel this, because he smiles at me and says, "Well, go on then."

So I kick off my trainers, roll my dungarees up to my knees and wade in so I am level with Dog. He looks at me, barks, then looks out to the waves and barks again as if to say, "okay then, let's play."

Dog is better at this game than me; he leaps high and clear of each wave and looks like he could do it all day long. After only three, I am breathing hard and have to limit myself to leaping every second wave. Then Dad is standing on the other side of Dog, his trousers rolled up like mine, and now there are three of us, wet to the bum and jumping waves and barking and laughing for all we are worth.

I don't know how long we jump for, but a lot of sea has passed beneath our feet and our paws before, one by one, we find stillness again. The three of us stand in the slow waves now, breathing hard and staring out towards the horizon. After a while, Dad slips the lead onto Dog's collar and we wander back to the rock, where we all rest and catch our breath – Dad and me sitting on the boulder, Dog stretched out at our feet. Dad keeps hold of Dog's lead, but he grips it lightly and Dog, for his part, seems content to lie and dry his fur in the last of the day's sun.

Mum still hasn't come to the cove, she hasn't felt this sand between her toes, and I think that if she were sitting with us now, then this moment would be perfect and complete.

Dad puts his hand on my knee and squeezes. He turns to me and smiles. And in that squeeze, I feel he is saying: *I know, Phyll. I know.*

21

Scattered Glass

Hilda laughing at me is nothing new. In fact, it's very old. It's how repetitive and boring it is that's most annoying.

But I tell myself: be like Dog. Jump this wave, let it pass beneath your feet.

I'm working on my necklace for Mum, using Jody's tools to file down the rough edges on my best bits of glass. Right now I'm concentrating on the red piece that Clark gave to me at the cove. This piece will sit in the centre of the necklace – it's the most important piece of all, so I'm being extra-specially careful.

But it's hard to concentrate with Hilda and the Horribles sniggering at me.

They are huddled over something – it's hidden beneath the table – and they whisper and point their faces at me, as if daring me to ask what's so funny. But whatever it is, it won't be funny; it will simply be annoying.

I'm doing a good job of ignoring them – of jumping the waves – until Hilda says something that turns my head. What she says is this:

"Poor Hedgehog."

And when she says it, she smirks.

I turn to face her. "What did you say?"

"Nothing," she says. And then she adds, "Hedge-hog."

The name Mum and Dad call me. The name *no one* else knows.

"What are you on about, Hilda?" I say it with as much bravery as I can, but something isn't right about this and I feel as if the room is slowly tilting, as if everything is about to come crashing down.

"What's that?" I say, pointing to whatever it is they have hidden under the table.

"Just a book. Found it on the floor."

"What book?"

But I have a horrible feeling that I know the answer to my question.

"It's about this girl," Hilda says. "Who believes in magic. Honestly, she's eleven and she believes in … genies!"

Hilda has my Book of Forts. I carry it in my bag so that if an idea comes to me I can write it down straight away. And now Hilda has it. My heart is beating fast and my face is hot. But I keep my voice calm.

"You went in my bag," I say.

But Hilda ignores me.

"Oh, and she has a crush on this boy," says Hilda, laughing. "But that's even more ridiculous than believing in genies."

You can handle them, Clark said when I not-exactly joked he was leaving me to the mercy of Hilda and the Horribles. Easy for him to say, harder for me to actually do with Hilda reading from my book of most personal thoughts, worries and hopes.

"Stop it," I say, trying to make myself sound as brave as I can.

But my words are quiet and unconvincing and they bounce off Hilda's smug confidence. Clark's seashell bracelet was meant to inspire fear in my enemies, but against Hilda it's as weak and useless as my voice.

"You can't blame her, though," Hilda says. "Her mother's mental, you see. She locks herself up in her room and cries all the time. So it's no wonder this girl's a bit weird."

At the mention of my mother I feel as though someone has knocked me to the floor, as if all the air has gone from my body. I try to say something, but the only words that come out are, "Don't…" and my voice is small.

"What's that? Don't what, Phyllis? Or should I say, *Hedgehog*?"

Tears swell in my eyes and spill over onto my cheeks. "Give it back."

"This?" she says, finally revealing my book. "What, is it yours?" Hilda says this in an innocent voice, as if she didn't know all too well whose it was.

"Give it back. Now."

"Or what?" says Hilda. "You'll set your genie on me?"

I drop my eyes to the table and see that the piece of red sea glass is wet and shiny. And as I stare at it, another fat tear rolls off the tip of my chin and onto the table.

This is the wave I couldn't jump; it's rolled over me and flowed through me.

"Oh boo hoo," says Hilda. And when I look at her again, she is blurred behind the tears that are streaming from my eyes. She goes to say something else but one of the Horribles – her name is Daisy – says in a quiet but firm voice. "Stop it, Hilda."

Hilda's head swivels towards her friend. "What?"

Daisy shrugs apologetically. "Give her book back," she says. "Before she drowns."

Hilda frowns at her with a mixture of confusion and annoyance. As if no one has ever before told her what to do. For a moment, the two girls stare at each other, then – with a huff – Hilda skims the book across the table.

"What's wrong with you?" I say.

"Me?" she says. "I'm not the one who believes in genies."

I look down at my hands. At Clark's bracelet made from shells. It may not frighten Hilda the way a necklace of bird bones might, but as I stare at the tiny shells I imagine Clark standing at my side. And picturing him there, I feel a surge of bravery.

"And I'm not the one with a cry-baby for a mummy," says Hilda.

And it's instant.

All the hurt and tears and nerves are replaced with a flash of anger.

"Don't!" I say, and my voice is loud and clear and strong. "Don't you *dare* talk about my mum! *Ever!*"

I'm not pretending now and Hilda can sense it. The way animals can sense fear, they can also sense its opposite.

Even though there's a table between us – and it's a good thing too, otherwise I would probably have

pushed Hilda over – Hilda takes a step away from me.
I stare hard into her eyes until she looks away. The way
a small yappy dog will when confronted with a stronger
animal.

"Baby," she says, but she has the good sense to walk
away as she says it.

One of the Horribles goes, but the other – Daisy –
stays.

"Your glass," Daisy says, pointing.

And when I follow her eyes, I see that my sea glass
is scattered all over the floor. I must have bumped the
table when I jumped up to shout at Hilda.

I get down on my knees to gather up the pieces, and
Daisy – without saying another word – does the same.

Fort #49

The lock on my Book of Forts isn't a real lock, not like one you get on a bike or a door, it's just a toy thing really. And now – thanks to Hilda – it's broken. I feel sad about that, but not as upset as I am about H (I don't even want to write her name any more. I don't want to waste the ink on her) invading my private place and my personal thoughts.

I worried that I would feel silly using this book again knowing that H has read it.

That it wouldn't feel the same. But opening the book is like opening the door (even one with a broken lock) to a good friend.

And right now, I need all the friends I can get.

It's a strange thing, but I feel loneliest at Camp Sunshine, where (now that Clark has gone) there are seven other children and two supervisors. But I don't feel connected to them, not the way I feel connected to Clark. At Camp Sunshine, I am surrounded by people, but I *feel* alone.

In my room, though – with no one else for company – I don't feel so lonely.

Dad is downstairs watching a film and, even though we are in different rooms, I feel that we are together.

It's the same with me and Mr Djinn – he's not even in the same house, but we are close in my mind.

Like Dog, on the other side of Cliffside Village. I can't hold him or stroke him, but if I close my eyes I can still see Dog running and wagging and jumping waves.

Clark is miles and miles away at the top end of the country. He doesn't have a phone so I can't even call him. But I know he's there, I know he's a friend and I feel – even over all of those miles – that I am connected to him.

Maybe that's the opposite of loneliness – connectedness. If that's even a word.

And I think it's love that keeps you connected, that stops you feeling lonely.

Not romantic kissy love, necessarily. But friendship and trust and ... just love. Plain and simple love running in two directions, from you to them and them to you. I love Dad and I know he loves me. And there is something similar with Mr Djinn, with Dog, with Clark. What we feel for each other – friendship and love – it runs both ways.

But with Mum, sometimes it feels as if that love runs only one way. I know she loves me, of course, but that love is closed up inside her sometimes, and when it's closed up like that it doesn't connect the way it should.

But I know it will pass. I know that she will come out again from under her cloud.

I think again about Dog, leaping wave after wave after wave. And life, I suppose, is like that. The waves are the problems and setbacks and disappointments that come at you one after the other — moving house, mean people, gone-away friends, sad family — and you have to face them full on and jump. You have to jump and bark and laugh while you do.

Because even waves change direction, even the strongest tide will eventually turn back towards the sea.

22
Tickety-Boo

I've used a lot of felt-tip pens in my life, but none quite as impressive as these – fat as broom handles with a tip as thick as my thumb. When I stab mine down onto the card, it leaves a red mark the size of a strawberry, completely covering the number below.

I've never played bingo before: I like it.

The man at the front of the room dips his hand into a round wire cage filled with what look like coloured ping-pong balls, except each one is printed with a number. Me and all the old folks watch as his hand pushes into the sea of balls.

In front of each of us is a card printed with rows of numbers. If the number on the ball matches a number on your card, you dab it with the marker pen. There are small prizes for getting a row of numbers and there is a big prize – a tartan-printed blanket – for the first person to dab off all the numbers on their card. It's more exciting than I would have believed.

We watch as the man's fingers close around a single ball and pull it from the cage. We strain to see if we can peep at the number between his fingers. But the man knows what he's doing and hides the ball in his hand. He leans towards his microphone.

"Tickety-boo," says the man, and already, before he even calls the number, I hear two markers thunk down onto the cards. "Sixty-two," says the man.

This is the other thing about bingo – the numbers all come with a rhyme or a code. *Two ducks in a row* is 22 because each '2' looks a little like a duck. *Dirty Gertie* is 30, because it rhymes. And if you know the code, you can mark off the lines more quickly. I don't know the code.

The man reaches again into the cage of balls.

"Ready?" says Mr Djinn. He looks pale today and his voice is croaky from all the coughing, which seems to be getting worse.

"Ready," I tell him.

Around the room, people glance downwards at their cards, holding in their minds the numbers they still need to dab. Well, some of us do. Some of the old folks stare off into space, some need a carer to help them, at least two are sleeping even though the room is bright with late afternoon sunshine.

The man pulls a blue ball from the cage. He dips his head towards his microphone, but doesn't speak yet – he waits, drawing out the excitement for a moment, and then, "Two fat ladies."

Despite looking so tired and creaky today, Mr Djinn moves with surprising speed, thudding his marker onto his card.

"Eighty-eight," says the man.

At the same time, Mr Djinn shouts "Line!", then he begins to cough, loud and hard. It takes him a moment to stop, and when he reaches for his water, his hand is quite trembly.

"Are you okay?" I ask.

"Of course, child. I just got a little excited."

The bingo man comes over to check Mr Djinn's card, and after seeing that, yes, he does have a line, he gives Mr Djinn his prize – a packet of chocolate biscuits. As the man walks back to the stage, one of the carers announces that we will have a short "comfort break" before carrying on. A comfort break, I have learned, is another kind of code. In this case it means going to the toilet, and several old folks are wheeled away by carers.

Mr Djinn does not at this moment require any "comfort".

"But I will have a biscuit," he says. "And so must you."

"Why is number '88' two fat ladies?" I ask.

"Imagine a letter eight with legs and a head," he says, and he wiggles his hands in the air, palms together, as if running them around the sides of a big number eight, or, perhaps…

"A fat lady!" I say.

"The best kind," says Mr Djinn.

"Excuse me?"

"My favourite wives were the fat ones," he says. "They were the most comfortable. And often the better cooks."

"Wives," I repeat. "As in more than one?"

"I am thousands of years old, child. Of course more than one."

"You look sad," I tell him.

"When you live a long time, many who are close to you will die. I have left flowers at the graves of twelve wives, and I miss every one of them. Even the skinny one."

"You must have a lot of children."

Mr Djinn shakes his head. "Genies can't have children. The reason, I don't know. Perhaps because we never were children ourselves."

"You were never a child? Wait, how is that possible?"

"We simply appear," says Mr Djinn, "whole and fully grown."

"Isn't that confusing?"

"I don't remember being confused. But there is a lot I do not remember. Would you care for another biscuit?"

I have so many questions, but I also have a feeling the answers would simply lead to more questions. So I let the matter drop and accept Mr Djinn's offer of a biscuit.

"You're very good at bingo," I say.

Mr Djinn laughs. "The competition isn't so challenging." He casts his glance across the room, taking in the sleeping bingo players.

"'Ah, to sleep,'" he says, "'perchance to dream.' Do you know who said that?"

I shake my head.

"William Shakespeare. The greatest writer ever to live. Unfortunately, I slept through his work."

"At the theatre?" I say.

"In a bottle. I slept through Mister Shakespeare's entire lifetime, which is a shame as I should have liked to see him very much."

"How long did you sleep?"

"That time, perhaps two hundred years, maybe

less. I woke in time for Mozart, though, so I should not complain."

"Two hundred years? Asleep?"

"Being a genie is tiring work. And soon" – he smiles now, a broad grin that shows his white teeth and lifts his eyes – "I will sleep for ever." His smile when he says this is the sort of smile Dad might make when he says he's going to have a glass of wine. Like it is something he is very much looking forward to.

But to me, this idea sounds terrible, and I feel a lump come to my throat and tears start in my eyes. Mr Djinn takes hold of my hand and squeezes it in his. "Don't cry, Phyllis. This is how the world works. 'All that lives must die', as Mister Shakespeare said. Why do you think all these oldies are sleeping on their bingo cards?"

"Because they're tired," I sniff.

Mr Djinn laughs. "Well that is true. But also…" He holds up a finger the way teachers do when they want you to pay attention, when what they have to say is important. "They are practising, child. For after."

"After what?"

"After life, of course. For the longest and most peaceful sleep they will ever know."

The bingo man clears his throat at the front of the room, and all the old folks are back in their chairs, fat markers in their hands. Those that are awake, anyway.

"Now dry your eyes and pay attention," says Mr Djinn. "I think we have a good chance of winning that tartan blanket."

23
The Caves

When Dad and I went to collect Dog today, the poor thing was again chained to his pole outside. I asked Dad if he thought Dog lived outside all the time, and he said that he probably did.

"Lots of dogs do," Dad said. "It's why they have fur coats."

But it didn't make me feel any better about it.

Dad is waiting in a pub called The Spyglass while I take Dog for his walk.

He said he would walk with me if I wanted, but the truth is, I want to do this on my own. With no one else saying we should turn left or right, or go home, or keep walking, or whatever. No one asking questions. Also, I think Dad really wanted to have a pint of beer, on *his* own. Probably for the same sorts of reasons.

So it's just me and Dog.

I pat him on the meaty part of his back leg that Dad says is called his haunch. Dog must have been rolling in the mud or something because his fur is extra dirty and matted today. Even his biscuit-shaped patch is hidden behind all the muck.

Dog is all forwards, pulling me along behind him, frustrated at how slow I am. Sometimes, especially when we go down a hill, I have to run to keep up. Of course, Dog is taking us to the beach and, when we reach the steps, he is pulling so hard I feel that either his lead will snap or he will drag me face-first all the way to the bottom.

There's nothing else for it: I unclip his lead.

And the minute I do, Dog tears away at full speed.

By the time I reach the cove, he is nowhere in sight. There is a scattering of people on the beach, some with dogs and one man flying a kite, but there is no sign of Dog. Probably he's digging behind a rock somewhere, or chasing some unfortunate creature.

I call his name, and when Dog doesn't come running I call it again, aware of how weird I must look walking along the beach and shouting out the word "Dog!"

I walk the full length of the cove and still there's no sign of Dog, so I call him again, not caring at all about the funny looks I'm getting. I cup my hands around my mouth, fill my lungs with air and shout again.

"*Dooooog*!!!"

But there is still no sign of him.

Remembering how he ran into the waves last time we were here, I begin walking along the shoreline and looking out across the waves to see if I can spot his shaggy head above the water. But he isn't there.

A terrible thought occurs to me. *What if he's drowned?*

I'm beginning to panic and I can feel my heart beating hard inside my chest. There is a lady nearby, carrying her shoes in her hand and staring out to sea as the waves wash over her feet. I run over to her.

"Excuse me, have you seen a dog?"

The lady turns towards me, then stares at me for a second before answering. "I've seen several," she says. "But if you ask me, they shouldn't be allowed down here, fouling all over the sand. If you ask me..."

I turn away from the lady, casting my eyes out across the cove. I run towards the kite flyer and ask him if he's seen a dog. The man barely takes his eyes off his kite. He laughs. "Not unless it can fly," he says, then laughs again at his own joke.

I run from person to person asking them the same question, but no one has seen a dog without an owner. And with every person who says "no", my panic grows and hardens until I can feel it like a fist in my tummy.

The last man I speak to asks if I've looked in the caves. He points towards the far side of the cove where the rocks rise out of the sea all jagged and black and tumbled together.

I run towards the caves, shouting "Dog!" at the top of my lungs and I'm almost there when my cries are answered by a joyous *bark bark bark*!

And I just know it's him.

I don't see him yet, but when I call his name again, he barks once more in reply.

I slow my run to a walk, still heading towards the caves, still calling Dog, still listening out for his yappy, growly bark.

Then ... it's confusing ... before I see Dog, I see a man emerge from behind a tumbled pile of rocks and boulders. He has a lead in his hand, the dog is still hidden from view, but you can tell by the shape of the man's body, the effort of his face, that the dog is pulling hard.

The man nearly slips on the wet rocks. "Steady," he says in a firm voice. "Steady."

The dog answers – a growly, yappy, excited bark – and then I see him. Mucky and scruffy and waggy and fine.

It's Dog.

I recognize the man too – I recognize his sunglasses and small beard that makes him look like a TV bad guy. I saw him on the beach when I first came down here on my own. But what is he doing with Dog – *my Dog* – on his lead?

"Hello," says the man, as if this is all completely normal. "We've met before, haven't we?"

I nod. I say, "Yes."

Dog is straining at the lead this man must have clipped to his collar. The man gives the lead a short sharp tug, and Dog relaxes. "Good boy," says the man. "Good boy."

"He's called Dog," I say, and the man tilts his head sideways as if examining me more carefully.

He pushes his sunglasses back on his head and blinks as his eyes adjust to the sunlight. His eyes are light blue, and without the sunglasses he looks a lot less like a TV baddie. "He's yours?"

"Yes. Well, not exactly. I walk him for someone else."

"I see," says the man. He squats down and very gently strokes the scratty fur between Dog's ears. "Found this chap digging about in the caves," he says. "Tide's coming in, though. If he stayed there much longer, he could have been ... well, trapped."

"Oh, I ... he ran away."

The man nods. "Dogs tend to," he says with a smile. "We were just about to try and find his owner, but it looks like you found us first."

The man holds out his hand, and it's obvious he wants me to give him my lead, which I do. The man takes Dog by the collar, then switches his lead for mine before handing it, and Dog, back to me.

"My name's Clive," he says.

"I'm Phyllis."

"Well, Phyllis, it was a pleasure to meet you." He laughs. "And Dog."

"Where's yours?" I ask him.

"Mine?"

"Your dog?"

"That, Phyllis, is a very good question." Clive shields his eyes with a hand and looks out across the cove. "If I'm not mistaken," he says, "that's him foraging around in all that scrub over there. See?"

I look in the direction the man is pointing, but I can't make out his dog.

"Right," says the man, pushing his sunglasses back down over his eyes, "I'd best go and get him before he eats something nasty. Take care, Phyllis. Take care of Dog."

"Yes," I tell him. "I will."

Dog, after I've clipped him onto his lead, still wants to run in the sea, but I'm not taking any more chances with him, so I keep his lead attached and wade out into the waves with him. Standing up to my knees in the water, and holding the lead with both hands, I must look kind of ridiculous but, so long as I have Dog I really don't care. By the time we head back to collect Dad, we are dripping with sea water, leaving two wet footprints and twice as many paw prints behind us on the dry pavement.

Dad has a packet of crisps and a bottle of lemonade waiting for me, and my arms are so tired I let Dad hold the lead as we walk back to Dog's house. I tell Dad about our walk, eat crisps and feed every fifth one to Dog. When I tell Dad about the caves, he nods and says we should avoid the beach for a while and stick to places where we won't need a boat to rescue him. I feel bad for Dog, but I know Dad's right.

Dog's owner, when he comes to the door, is smoking a cigarette, which he doesn't take from between his lips when he speaks.

"Thought you'd got lost."

"Sorry," I say, "we were jumping in the waves. I hope that's okay?"

The man shrugs. "Makes no difference to me."

I hold out the lead, but as the man reaches out to take it, Dog shrinks back against my legs.

"C'm'ere," the man says around his cigarette. And he grabs the lead and yanks Dog roughly towards him.

"Easy," says Dad and, for a moment, the man and my dad meet eyes and stare at each other. It's quite dramatic. Then the man looks away and begins leading Dog towards the back garden.

"Also," says Dad, "you might want to get a tag for his collar."

"A tag?"

"In case he gets lost," Dad says.

The man turns to look at Dad, squinting at him through the smoke rising from his cigarette. "Make me an offer," he says.

Dad frowns. "An offer?"

"For the mutt. You care so much about him, make me an offer. How does fifty quid sound?"

Dad is taken aback by this. "We're not ... I'm sorry, it's just ... the timing isn't..."

The man snorts. "Twenty, then. Can't even get a bottle of whiskey for that."

"We're not buying a dog right now," Dad says.

Right now?

"Fine," says the man. "Take him. Just take him."

I look at Dad's face. I can see him thinking about this offer of a free dog. All he has to do is nod his head and Dog is ours. We could buy him a bowl and a basket and give him a bubble bath. He could be sleeping on my bed *tonight*.

All Dad has to do is say yes.

Dad shakes his head. "We can't," he says. Then he turns to me. "We can't, sweetheart. I'm sorry."

"All bark," says the man, "and no bite."

24
A Postcard

I looked on a map to see how far away Edinburgh is from Gran and Granddad's house in Skye, and it turns out Scotland is a lot bigger than I'd realized. In his auntie's house, Clark is over 200 miles from my grandparents. Almost as far away as he is from Corsair's Cove. And when I realized that, it made me miss him even more.

But here it is, a postcard from 373 miles away.

On the front is a picture of a castle, with a man standing in front of it wearing a kilt, fancy socks and a fluffy hat. He's playing some Scottish pipes that look very complicated.

Clark's handwriting is surprisingly neat. The lines are straight and none of the letters are smudged:

Hello Phyll!

Scotland is not as bad as I'd thought, they've even got a beach that we go to most days. Guess what, I found some sea glass which I'll bring back for you. Two red bits and

a really nice green one. My cousins are okay too, but they keep teasing me for my accent, which is ridiculous because I sound completely normal compared to them. I ate haggis yesterday – I would tell you what's in it, but you might barf. Anyway, hope you are okay and hope you're enjoying Camp "Sunshine" without me. I'm sure you are.

See you.

Clark.

PS. If your hair has grown enough, maybe you can use this.

The postcard came in an envelope, which, as well as the postcard, contained a tartan patterned hair clip. And it turns out my hair is – just – long enough to hold the slide. I wear it while I sit in my bedroom and write a two-sided letter back to Clark, telling him all about Dog, his grumpy owner and the man with sunglasses who found Dog in the caves.

It's only when I've finished that I realize Clark didn't include a return address. So I fold the letter carefully and tuck it into the back of my Book of Forts. Maybe I'll give it to him when he comes back. Whenever that might be.

Fort #50

I love my hair clip – it's a small thing, and I'd never have chosen it for myself. I think that's what makes it so good. It's something I never would have had if it wasn't for Clark. But now that I have it, it feels right and it feels like it was meant to be mine.

A bit like Clark. I think he was meant to be mine too.

"They belong together" is a thing I've heard people say, when they're talking about two people who are best friends, or who are in love. I think it's nice to belong to someone in that way. And to know they belong to you.

Like Mum and Dad. They belong to each other. And Gran and Granddad. And Mr Djinn – if you believe his stories – he belonged to twelve different wives.

But belonging is different to being *owned*. The way Mr Djinn was owned – again, if you believe the stories – by the men and women who held him as a genie. Being owned like that means you have no freedom. It means someone else controls you. Someone else can treat you however they want.

Dog is owned by the man who speaks with a cigarette in his mouth.

But I don't think he belongs with him.

Belonging is being where you are supposed to be. And Dog belongs with someone who loves him.

Everybody does.

25

A Handsome Chap

"Who's a handsome chap?" says Mr Djinn.

"Who's handsome?" repeats the parrot. And then it says it again. "Who's handsome?"

From outside, the pet shop is narrow and to look at it you wouldn't imagine there was room inside for much more than mice, stick insects and a few fish. But once you step through the single door, the shop goes back into a wide, open space heaving with rabbits, guinea pigs, tortoises, lizards and dozens and dozens of birds.

Earlier today, we were sitting outside Ocean Breeze old folks' home, looking down on the cove, when Mr Djinn said, "All this walking, Phyllis, must have made your legs very strong."

"Stronger than they were," I told him.

"Strong enough to push an old man in a wheelchair?" asked Mr Djinn.

"You mean you?"

"I mean me," said Mr Djinn. "After all this dog walking, I thought, perhaps, you might walk me."

"Where would you like to go?"

A gull circled overhead and squawked his nonsense before floating on the breeze out towards the sea.

"Parrots," said Mr Djinn. "I would like to go and see parrots."

So we came here. To the pet shop.

Chloe, the friendly carer from the home, made me phone Dad first to get permission. Dad asked to speak to Chloe. And, as the pet shop is literally over the road from the old folks' home, Dad said it would be fine — just so long as I didn't come home with any hamsters.

Mr Djinn dips his hand down the side of his wheelchair and produces a packet of Brazil nuts. He pokes a nut through the wire of the parrot's cage and the parrot snatches it away with its beak.

"Such manners," says Mr Djinn. "Not so much as a 'thank you'?"

"Not so much," says the parrot.

"Does it understand?" I ask.

"They only mimic, repeat, copy," Mr Djinn says, then he laughs as if remembering something. "Blackbeard's parrot used to say the most terrible words."

"You mean swear words?"

"Oh yes. That bird's language was more colourful than his feathers. Pirates, as perhaps you can imagine, speak in a most rough manner. And so Blackbeard's parrot did the same."

Mr Djinn passes a nut to me, I hold it out to the cage and the parrot plucks it from my fingers.

"What the parrot says is simply noise," says Mr Djinn. "The squawkings, if you like, of a small-brained animal. And, as you will learn, some people are the same."

My mind flashes onto Hilda, and to Dog's owner. It is easy to imagine them both as squawking, flapping, small-brained creatures.

"Small brained," says the parrot. "Small brained."

"Exactly," says Mr Djinn, and he feeds the bird another nut.

"Well look at that," says a voice behind us. "A talking parrot."

I turn to see a lady approaching the birdcages. She is accompanied by an adorable Yorkshire terrier.

"Shall we say hello to the birdies?" says the old lady, and her dog woofs as if saying, *Yes, let's do that.*

The terrier looks remarkably like Tim from the lost dog poster – the same teddy bear ears, bushy eyebrows and light brown moustache. Of course most Yorkshire terriers look like this, but something is very familiar about this one … maybe it's his hopeful eyes.

"He's very friendly," says the lady, and there is something familiar about her too. "He doesn't bite," she says, and I realize that it's her voice. I've heard it before. On the phone.

"I…"

"Yes, dear?"

"Is…" I point to the Yorkshire terrier. "Is he called Tim? Timmy?"

The lady's eyebrows rise above the frames of her glasses. "Why yes," she says. "Yes it is – wait, are you…?"

"Phyllis," I say.

"Well, I'll be," says the lady. "The girl on the phone."

I nod. "So it is Timmy? You got him back?"

"Yes," says the lady. "I got him back." And then she hugs me.

Mr Djinn clears his throat. "Phyllis," he says, "perhaps you might introduce me to your friend?"

26

Found

Two doors along from the pet shop is a bakery called Victoria's Sponge, where Mr Djinn insists on buying a slice of cake for each of us.

I text Dad to ask if this is okay, and he texts back that it's fine, so long as I don't bring any old folk home and he adds one of those laughing faces.

The lady is called Nora and, once we are seated at a table by the window, she tells us how, after my phone call, she went around replacing all the soggy lost dog posters with new ones covered in plastic.

"And this time," she says. "I offered a reward."

"And I assume" – Mr Djinn glances at Timmy, sitting at Nora's feet and begging for cake with his eyes – "that someone called?"

Nora dabs her mouth with a napkin. "A man. Two days later."

Mr Djinn nods. "I expect he was curious to know the full extent of the reward."

"That's right," says Nora. "So I suggested twenty-five pounds, which I thought was rather generous."

"I would agree," says Mr Djinn. "But, this man, I suspect he did not find it so generous?"

"That's exactly right. He said—"

"May I guess?" says Mr Djinn.

Nora sits back in her chair and gives Mr Djinn a quick once-over with her eyes, as if trying to get the measure of this strange old man. She smiles and takes another forkful of cake.

Mr Djinn says, "The man suggested that if the reward were larger, say fifty pounds, then he might be motivated to venture outside and search for little Timmy?"

Nora claps her hands together as if Mr Djinn had just performed some sort of trick. Which I suppose he has. "Exactly," she says. "Exactly so."

"So you agreed?" I ask. "To pay fifty pounds?"

"I did." Nora bends down and scoops Timmy up, sitting him in her lap. "I'd have paid anything in the world."

"In which case," says Mr Djinn, "I'd say you got a bargain."

Timmy strains against Nora's hands, attempting to get at her slice of cake.

"Cake's no good for you," Nora whispers into the dog's ear.

Timmy yaps, as if to say: *It's no good for you either, but you're eating it.*

Or at least, that's how it sounds to me. And maybe it does to Nora too, because she sighs.

She says, "Okay, but only a *teensy* bit." And she feeds Timmy a small bite of her cake.

Mr Djinn clears his throat. "Regarding the most generous reward you offered this man. How long until he *found* your dog?"

"He called the very next day," says Nora. "Called to arrange a – a 'rendezvous', he called it. Suggested we meet in a garden centre car park."

"Of course," says Mr Djinn.

"What are you saying?" asks Nora. "Do you suspect it was some form of ruse?"

"What's a ruse?" I ask.

"A dishonest endeavour," says Mr Djinn. "A scheme, a con, a plot."

"Wait," I say. "Are you suggesting this man had Timmy all along?"

"I suspect so," says Mr Djinn.

"So this man tricked me?" says Nora. "He ... stole from me?"

Mr Djinn nods. "And I fear you are not the only victim. I read in the newspaper that there have been many such *dog-nappings*."

Nora puts a hand to her chest. "How ... how simply dreadful."

"It is an old trick, but no less unpleasant for it. I suspect this man takes lost dogs – perhaps even dogs who are not lost – purely for the purpose of raising and then claiming a reward."

"Did you get a look at him?" says Mr Djinn. "This man?"

"Not exactly," says Nora. "He was jolly tall, but he was wearing one of those caps and a pair of sunglasses."

"Indeed," says Mr Djinn. "Indeed."

"Were you ever a policeman?" asks Nora.

"I was many things," says Mr Djinn, his eyes twinkling. "But, as far as I can recall, I never worked for the police."

"As far as you recall!" says Nora, laughing as if Mr Djinn has just made a joke.

And then, like a parrot repeating a phrase that has taken its fancy, she says it again.

27

Water Everywhere

Dad said he thought my idea was a good one. But he warned me not to get my hopes up. Mum might be tired, he said. She might find it too stressful. In which case, we would need to think of a plan B.

My idea being this:

Bring Dog back to our house. Not to live, not to stay, just to have a massive bubble bath in the paddling pool.

Turns out plan B is not needed.

Mum came into the garden as we were filling the paddling pool, Dog running around the garden, barking at bees and leaping at butterflies. Mum came down in her pyjamas to see what all the noise was. We introduced her to Dog and, when Mum squatted down to say hello, Dog calmly rolled over to have his belly tickled.

"He's adorable," Mum said in a quiet voice. "And, oh my lord, *very* stinky."

"We're going to bathe him," I said, nodding at the by now half-full paddling pool.

"That," said Mum, "sounds like a tremendous idea. I'll go and get changed."

"Great," said Dad, "I'll leave you two to it."

"Why, where are you going?"

"Shed," Dad said. "Man stuff."

And Mum just looked at me and rolled her eyes. "Men love sheds," she said. "You'll learn this and many other mysteries when you get older."

So Dad disappeared into the shed to work on his secret project, I continued filling the pool, and Mum went inside to get changed. Except now she is dripping in dirty soapy bubbles.

"He's so friendly," Mum says from the edge of the pool. "Aren't you, boy? You're *sooo* friendly."

Dog answers by jumping up and turning a full circle in the air before landing with a gigantic splash.

"I always had dogs as a girl," she says.

"When will Josie have her puppies, Mum?"

"I don't know. Shall we call Gran and Granddad later and find out?"

"Yes please."

"Come on then, let's finish washing this pooch."

She squirts a dollop of shampoo into my hands and I work it into the fur of Dog's back legs. The water in the pool is quite brown now, but Dog smells about a million times better and his biscuit-coloured patch is more obvious than ever.

"You're going to need a very long bath yourself," Mum says to me.

She swirls her hands in the water and scoops out a small mountain of foam, which she blows high into the air. Dog jumps and yaps, snapping his teeth at the multi-coloured bubbles. Mum tickles the wet fur between his shoulder blades.

"He's thin," she says. "Aren't you, boy?"

Dog shakes his head, flapping his ears from side to side and showering Mum with water.

"I think you offended him," I say.

"Maybe he'd like some leftovers," Mum says. "There's some chicken in the fridge. Would Dog like that?"

Mum definitely speaks Dog, or Dog certainly speaks Mum, because he barks excitedly and nearly scrambles over the side to get at Mum in his excitement.

"I think that's a yes," Mum says. "Would you like some chicken?"

Dog makes another lunge for Mum. He leaps high, landing with his paws on the edge of the pool.

"Okay," Mum says. "I'll go and get the chicken."

Dog begins clambering up over the edge, his back legs thrashing in the water and his front paws, his front *claws*, pressing hard into the soft rubber sides of my paddling pool.

And, really, it's all so inevitable.

I watch in horror as Dog continues trying to scrabble over the side of a pool that was designed to contain up to four children, not one highly excitable dog. He has a firm hold on the sides with his front paws, then brings up one back leg then the other so that – for a moment – he is balanced on the edge of the paddling pool like a cat on a fence.

And then it all goes wrong.

There is a noise like a huge fart – long and high and rippling – and this is quickly joined by a second, a third and a fourth fart as Dog's claws rip through the side of my paddling pool. The noise grows in volume, water begins to swell up around Dog's feet, but, miraculously, he is still perched on top of the ruined pool.

For a second.

Then the entire thing – there's really no other word for it – explodes.

Water erupts in all directions, shooting in a spectacular and perfect circle all over the garden, all over Mum, and all over me.

For the briefest of moments Dog is suspended in mid-air before he comes thudding down onto the wet lawn.

Mum is still laughing about it an hour and a half later when we tell the story to Gran and Granddad on the computer.

She chuckles while I'm brushing my teeth for bed, holding her fingers under the tap and flicking me with water.

And after she has read two chapters of *Treasure Island*, after she has tucked me in and kissed my nose, I hear her downstairs, laughing with Dad.

Fort #51

Mum, when she saw me in my swimming costume today, she said, "What's happened to your legs, Phyllis?" – and the way she said it, all surprised and a bit shocked, I thought maybe I'd cut my knee or something without noticing. Then she squeezed my leg above the knee and said, "You've got muscles, Phyllis. Where on Earth did they come from?"

And I blushed and shrugged and said I didn't know. But, thinking about it now, I suppose they came from walking up and down 461 steps to get to the cove. Sometimes trying to keep up with a very strong and pully dog. All that exercise would put muscles on a pencil.

Not that they're big muscles. I haven't all of a sudden got weightlifter's legs. They're just a tiny bit stronger than they were before we moved here. A little more meaty in the leg and a little less knobbly in the knee.

But it has made me think...

We laughed a lot today, me and Mum and Dad. And it was like I had my old mum back – from before the time when all the clouds came in. We laughed so much that it made my tummy muscles ache. Like your legs ache when you've done lots of exercise.

And that's when the thought came to me.

Maybe happiness is like a muscle too.

And maybe laughing is how you exercise it.

How you make your Happy stronger.

I don't know how exactly I'm going to make Mum laugh again like she did today – I'm not very good at jokes, and I don't have another paddling pool to burst – but Dog seems to know the trick. And if that's not a good excuse to bring him around more often, then I don't know what is.

28

When One Friend Meets Another

"I had a tiger once," Mr Djinn says.

In the company of Mr Djinn – and all these other old folks – Dog is calm, as if he knows that is the appropriate way to be in this slow and quiet place. As if he, like me, can sense that Mr Djinn is particularly tired today.

After we collected Dog today, instead of dragging us to the beach, Dog turned the other way, dragging me and Dad straight back to our house. He was filthy with mud again, from sleeping outside in all the rain, probably, and in much need of another bath. The problem, of course, was that the bath – our paddling pool – was now in tatters. "We'll just have to shower him instead," Mum said. So that's what we did, with a hosepipe, a sponge and my strawberry shampoo. And if Dog likes a bath, he *loves* a shower. And after Mum had blow-dried him with her hair-drier, he looked so fluffy and adorable that I just had to show him off.

So I took him for a walk and brought him here to Ocean Breeze.

Dog sits between us, occasionally resting his chin on Mr Djinn's knee so my human friend can tickle my dog friend between the ears. The tartan blanket that he won at bingo is folded over Mr Djinn's legs and this somehow makes him look much older. Maybe not thousands of years old, but older than I have seen him look before.

"A real live tiger?" I say.

Mr Djinn takes a handkerchief from up his sleeve and coughs into it. Even coughing seems like an effort for him today. When he has finished coughing, he folds up the handkerchief and pushes it back inside his sleeve.

"Very much alive," says Mr Djinn. "But I couldn't keep him."

"Why not?"

"Tigers are not meant to be kept. Besides, they eat too much and they ruin your furniture."

One of the carers – the friendly one called Chloe – asks Mr Djinn if he would like a cup of coffee, but I've brought good coffee in a flask and Mr Djinn tells Chloe that he is fine, thank you very much. The lady strokes

Dog's fur and pats him on his biscuit-shaped patch. This is the second time she has asked Mr Djinn if he wants coffee and the second time he has said no. I think Chloe only came by so she could stroke Dog.

"He's so fluffy," she says. "And he smells of..." she takes a moment, "strawberries?"

"It's his shampoo," I tell her.

"You're *so* fluffy," she says again, before moving on with her tea trolley.

"Why did you have a tiger in the first place?" I ask. "If tigers aren't for keeping."

"I saved him," says Mr Djinn.

"What from?"

"Not what," says Mr Djinn, "but who? I saved him from bad men who sought to capture him and remove him from his natural home."

"Why would anyone do that?"

"For the same reason most wicked deeds are done. Money. There are people – also bad – who will pay a great deal for a tiger."

"And why would they do that?"

"Different reasons. But, ultimately, just to prove they can."

"To show off?"

"Precisely, child. You have put it perfectly."

An elderly lady shuffles up to us and asks what the dog's name is.

"Dog," I tell her.

"Yes," says the lady, "the dog."

"He's called Dog," I say.

"Well he's not a cat, is he? I'm eighty-four, you know. And I ought to know a dog when I see one."

"The dog," says Mr Djinn gently, "is called Dog. I think, perhaps, someone thought it was funny."

"Hmphh," says the lady, who obviously does not.

"I know," says Mr Djinn, and the lady softens.

"Well," she says patting Dog on the bottom, "you're a very attractive fellow." And she glances at Mr Djinn. I don't know if old people have crushes, but if they do, I'd say this lady has a crush on Mr Djinn. She pats Dog one more time before shuffling away.

"Did you use wishes?" I say.

"Excuse me, child. Wishes?"

"To rescue the tiger."

Mr Djinn shakes his head. "I used a very big knife and a fierce face. These things have their own magic."

Dog stretches, yawns and shakes his chops. Four chairs over, an old gentleman makes a sort of kissy noise at Dog then pats both knees with his hands. Dog trots over to investigate.

I sigh. "Because people can be so awful to animals," I say. "Dogs, tigers, whatever. And it's not like the animals did anything to deserve it."

"It is a sad truth, child. Some people do not have good hearts. They see the world as if it were filled with things for them to take and abuse and own. Animals, forests, rivers. People too."

"People?"

"Oh yes, and in many ways. It happened not far from here, you know."

"In Ocean Breeze?"

Mr Djinn shakes his head. "In Bristol, hundreds of years ago. People were sold for money and metal. Slaves, child, brought here and taken away on the most dreadful ships and treated no better than animals and often worse. A truly wretched and shameful cargo."

"Why did people do that?"

This is the third time in as many minutes that I have asked Mr Djinn to explain the selfish and cruel behaviour of people. This time he raises his eyebrows, as if inviting me to answer my own question.

"Money?"

"Correct," says Mr Djinn. "The greed of men is a terrible evil."

"But the sailors, why didn't they just refuse?"

"Many did. But … when there is money to be made, greedy men will go to great lengths and sink to low depths to ensure they make it."

"Like what?"

"When onshore, sailors like to do two things – they enjoy the company of ladies, and the refreshment of strong drink."

"Like beer?"

"Indeed. The owners of the slave ships encouraged the owners of the drinking houses to get the sailors extremely drunk."

"Encouraged how?"

"With money, child. What else? And so the sailor drinks more and more, and soon he drinks more than he can pay for. At which point he finds himself suddenly and inexplicably surrounded by strong men carrying big sticks and plenty of rope."

"Rope?"

"Something ship owners possess in abundance. And slave-ship owners even more so. And now our drunken sailor is presented with two choices: go to prison, or work on a ship, no matter how wretched, until his debt is paid."

"Couldn't they just run away?"

Mr Djinn laughs heartily at this. "I am sure many

tried. But running is not so easy with a belly full of beer and rum. A running sailor is soon a fallen sailor, and soon after that, he is bound in rope."

"That's awful."

"Indeed it is. Beware of men with rope, child. They are rarely up to anything good."

29

Looking Forwards

The picture on this postcard is of a dog – small, black, with grey whiskers and a funny little tartan hat.

> Dear Phyll,
>
> I saw this postcard and it made me think of you. I know you're mad for dogs and I thought you'd like this one. It's a Scottie dog. Which is probably why it's on the front of this postcard in a silly hat.
>
> I wonder if anyone called you yet about the dog walking. I bet you have loads by now. I can just picture you being dragged along the cove by, like, 100 dogs. Maybe when I get back I can help you. Oh yes, I'm coming back next week, so less than a week by the time you get this.
>
> Bye for noo (as they say in Scotland)
>
> Clark

Less than a week. That could be six days, or five or even four. It's so annoying that I don't have a phone number for Clark, but I guess I'll see him soon enough.

I turn the postcard over again to look at the picture of the little doggie in his tartan hat. Then I look again at Clark's handwriting, at his name, signed with a flourish, at the bottom.

Less than a week.

I can't wait.

30
A Man With Rope

After we give Dog his garden shower today, and after Mum blow-dries him into what is more or less a four-legged pom-pom, Dad drives us to the pet shop.

Six packets of dog treats, a new lead and a tartan collar comes to £24.00. I have brought a pocketful of money from my piggy bank, but when we reach the counter, Dad gets his wallet out to pay the lady.

But I want this collar, at least, to come from me, so that's how we divide it up. Dad pays for the treats and the lead, and I pay £11.99 for a new tartan collar with a silver name tag. I know Dog isn't Scottish, or even a Scottie dog, but I like the collar, and I think Dog does too.

"What do you want on the tag?" says the lady. "What's this young boy's name?"

"Dog," says Dad.

"Actually," I say, "I think it should be Dunk."

The lady looks confused.

"He looks like a new dog," I say to Dad. "Don't you think he deserves a proper name?"

"Well, I suppose so," says Dad. "But … what was the name you said?"

"Dunk," I say, patting him on his biscuit-shaped patch. "Don't you see?"

"It looks like a biscuit," Dad says. "That's brilliant."

"I know," I say. Which isn't very modest, but it is a brilliant name.

"Dunk," says the lady, clearly not as impressed as Dad. "D-U-N-K." She writes it down on a scrap of paper. "And a number?"

"Hang on," says Dad. "What if he goes missing and someone calls old misery guts saying they've found a 'Dunk'?"

"We'll use my number then. Anyway, misery guts probably wouldn't care if 'Dog' went missing. At least if someone calls me we can do something about it."

Dad considers this.

The lady behind the counter clears her throat. "Ahem?"

Dad nods, "Okay then."

"So it's Dunk?" says the woman.

"Yes," I say. "It's Dunk."

On the drive home, Dunk sits in the back seat next to me. He pushes his head out of the half-open window so that his fur ruffles and his ears flap in the breeze. As we approach home, we drive past the cove and Dog – *Dunk* – barks and yaps at the top of his voice. I say to Dad that Dunk wants a splash in the waves, so Dad drops us off and tells me to call him when we're ready to head back to old misery guts' house.

There is a chill in the air this evening, grey clouds in the sky, and the cove is quiet.

Dunk is less frantic than he was the first few times we came and, as the tide is a long way out, I let him off his lead so he can run and splash and explore. I place the lead in my backpack, along with his treats and a rubber bone that we bought at the last moment. I should feel happy, but I don't. I feel the exact opposite of happy.

I suppose that I love Dunk now. I love all dogs, but this is different. I love him properly. And the thought of him sleeping outside with a chain attached to his collar, hungry and unloved, it makes me so sad that before I know it, I can feel tears standing in my eyes.

No matter what Mr Djinn says, I'm no genie. And

I don't have a big knife or a fierce face. And even if I could rescue Dog from his mean owner, I can't offer him a home. But as I watch him run and bark and play in the waves, I can't help wondering if no home might be better than a bad home.

"Don't worry, Phyllis, it might never happen."

The mention of my name surprises me and I look up to see the man with the small beard and the sunglasses. Clive.

"Hello," I say.

"Haven't lost that dog of yours again, have you?"

I shake my head.

"So what's up?" Clive asks. His dog lead dangles by his side; it's a simple one made of plaited rope, which Clive winds around his hand as he talks.

I shrug. "Just stuff."

Clive lets the lead fall loose so it dangles alongside his leg, then he begins again to gather it up and wrap it around his hand again. Looking up at him from where I sit on the sand, he seems incredibly tall.

"Where's your dog?" I ask.

Clive looks out across the sand. "Out there somewhere," he says.

I realize that of the three times I have seen this man, I have never seen his dog.

"You walking Dog again?" And he chuckles at the mention of the name.

I'm about to tell him that Dog is now called Dunk but – as Clive lets his lead uncoil and drop to his side – Mr Djinn's words come back to me:

Beware of men with rope.

"No," I say to the man.

"Walking someone else's dog then?"

I shake my head. "I only walk the one."

"Right," says Clive. "I see." And again, he gathers up the lead.

And that's when Dunk comes bounding over. He stops in front of us and sits on the sand, a stick between his teeth, his tail brushing back and forth on the sand.

"Hello," says Clive, reaching down to pat Dunk on the head, and it's clear that he doesn't recognize him as the scruffy mutt formerly known as Dog.

"Where have you been?" says Clive, and he lets the lead, the lead I have never seen him use, hang loose again at his side.

And now I know – I just know – who is stealing dogs and holding them for ransom. But just to be sure, I hear myself saying, "Is this your dog?"

My heart is beating like crazy, but my voice is calm.

Clive lifts his sunglasses and stares at me, as if

searching my face for tell-tale signs that I know what he's up to. He holds my gaze for seconds, for what feels like a hundred hours, and I do my best to look relaxed, to look not-terrified, to not show that I know he is a horrible, evil dog-napper. Clive slides his sunglasses back down over his eyes.

"Yes," he says. "This is my dog." And he clips his lead onto Dunk's collar.

I should leave it at that. But I can't help myself and I say, "What's he called? Your dog?"

Clive squats down so he is level with Dunk. He pats him on the back of the neck, his fingers lingering over the new tartan collar. He wants to read the name on the silver tag, but he can't do it without giving away the fact that he doesn't know Dunk's name.

"Got a lot of questions today, haven't you?" he says.

Dog dips his head towards me and gruffs. I stroke his head.

"See for yourself," the man says. "It's on his collar."

And I have to admit, this is a clever move by Clive.

"Dunk," I say, reading the silver name tag that we bought less than one hour ago.

"That's right," says Clive, as if he'd known this all along. "Well, me and Dunk had best be on our way. You take care of yourself, Phyll."

The man begins to walk away, but Dunk turns back to me, tugging against the lead and making a low sorry bark. I can feel the tears coming to my eyes again, but I know I must hold them back, so I turn my face away from Dunk and Clive and look out across the churning waves.

"Here," says Clive in a gentle voice. "Here, boy."

From the corner of my eye, I see Clive pull something from his pocket and hold it out to Dunk. For a brief moment, I think it might be some kind of weapon, a club maybe, but when I turn to get a proper look, I see it is nothing more dangerous than a sausage.

"Here, Dunk," says the man. "Here."

Dunk takes the sausage, Clive leads him away and they disappear from sight.

I cry for maybe ten minutes – big, wet, snotty, shaky crying. I cry until my tummy aches and I'm exhausted. Then I pick up my bag and head for home.

31

You Did What!?

"You did what!?"

Mum and Dad say the exact same words at the exact same time.

"I let him take Dunk."

Dad puts his hands to his face.

Mum, whose hands are already on her face – like that painting of the man screaming – takes her hands away and places them on her hips. We are sitting in the kitchen; Mum and Dad at one side of the table, me at the other. Like they are police, perhaps, and I'm the bad guy.

I burst into tears. "I'm sorry."

They each reach a hand across the table, each tell me it's okay. With my hands in theirs I'm a bit stretched out and it's sort of uncomfortable. This idea, I don't know why, makes me chuckle. Maybe because I'm exhausted. Or maybe I'm going a little bit crazy.

"What is it?" Dad says.

"I'm a bit stretched out," I say.

And they let go of my hands.

"So," says Mum, her voice more steady now. "Talk."

I tell them again about the person napping dogs, I tell them about the man on the beach – Clive – who always has a lead but never has a dog. I tell them that if this man is the dog-napper – and I'm certain he is – then he will phone the number on Dunk's collar and ask for a reward. Then we can arrange a rendezvous, call the police, and the police will throw him in jail for dog-napping.

"Don't you think the police have better things to do?" says Dad.

"Actually," says Mum, "this isn't exactly the crime capital of the world, is it?"

"True," says Dad. "They might be glad of the action."

"What about the man?" Mum says. "Dog's real owner."

"Misery guts," says Dad.

"He's so mean to him," I say. "He makes him sleep outside. On a chain."

"Doesn't feed him much, either, by the look of it," says Dad. "Or walk him."

"Or love him," I say. "And I think … I think Dunk's scared of him."

Then I burst into tears, again.

"Okay," says Mum. "So what do we do now?"

"Dad ... Dad phones the man," I say, and my voice is all wet and shaky. "And tells him ... tells him we're keeping Dog. Keeping Dunk."

"What if he says no?"

"He won't," says Dad. "He already asked us to take him, but ... we said no."

Mum thinks about this. "Because of me?" she says. "Are you saying he could have been here now, if it wasn't for me?"

"That's not what I'm saying, no. The man sprung it on us, and it just wasn't ... the time wasn't right."

And now Mum has tears in her eyes too. "What if the man from the cove doesn't want a ransom?" she says. "What if he just wanted Dunk?"

"Then at least he'll have someone who wants him," I say.

Mum strokes my cheek with the back of her finger. She strokes it once, twice, three times. Then, with a small nod, she stands from the table and says, "Okay."

We have sausages and mash for supper, and after that I have a long soak in the bathtub. Mum comes up with me; she turns down the lights and sets four small candles flickering around the bath. "To help you relax," she says. And while I lie in the bath, Mum washes my hair. I can't remember the last time she did that. She sings quietly while she does it and, even though her voice isn't very good, and she can't remember the words to what she's singing, I lie there and listen to her until the water goes cold.

After my bath, Mum reads to me while I'm wrapped up in bed. But I'll have to ask her to read those pages again, because in no time at all, my eyelids fall closed and I'm asleep.

32

Dogs Have Wishes Too

For most of my visit today, Mr Djinn is never more than half awake. Mostly not even more than a quarter awake. Sometimes he dozes, his eyes drifting closed and his chin dropping to his chest. He mutters in his sleep, but his words are quiet, squished together, and sound like they're in a foreign language.

When he is awake we play a game of cribbage, and when he dozes, he holds my hand. He seems to know when the sleep is creeping up on him – he reaches out to take my hand, rests it on the arm of his chair, then his eyes close and he sleeps and nods and mutters in his strange language.

His eyes flick open now, and he smiles and picks up his cards.

"Whose turn is it?" he asks, his voice croaky.

"Mine," I tell him.

Mr Djinn smiles. "You would say that."

After I play my card, I pour a little coffee from my

flask into his cup. Mr Djinn waits until I've stopped pouring and put the flask down.

"Thank you, child," he says. "My own personal genie."

"Genies are meant to make things better," I say. "What if I made things worse?"

Mr Djinn was disappointed not to see Dunk today, although he didn't seem entirely surprised. Many of the other old folks were hoping to see him too. They have shuffled over to Mr Djinn's chair, hoping to say hello to Dunk, to stroke his fur and pat his biscuit-shaped patch. But Dunk is not here. The truth is, he could be anywhere.

Mr Djinn plays a card. "Six points."

I mark this down on the paper.

"Animals have wishes too," he says.

"Animals?"

"Mostly they wish for food. But sometimes, too many times, they wish to be free. To escape. To be safe. They wish for love, also. Dogs in particular wish to be loved."

I play my card, but score no points. Even half asleep, Mr Djinn is way better at this game than me. It doesn't help that I'm finding it hard to concentrate.

My mind is filled with thoughts of Dunk, where he is now and what he's doing. If he's happy, or scared, or hungry. If he's being treated well and walked.

"He will be fine," Mr Djinn says sleepily. "All will be fine."

"But how can you be sure? How can y—"

And then my phone rings: *Caller unknown.*

It has to be the man.

Last night after I told Mum and Dad about my plan, Mum said she didn't like the idea of me answering the phone to a criminal. So I promised that if any unknown numbers came up, I would give my phone to Mum or Dad to answer, or if I was on my own, let the caller leave a message. We didn't discuss what I'd do if I was with Mr Djinn.

"Perhaps I should answer that," he says, holding out his hand for my phone.

He accepts the call and turns on the phone's speaker so I can hear.

"Hello," says Mr Djinn, "who is this?"

"Have you lost a dog?" says the man. I recognize his voice as the man from the beach.

"Why yes," says Mr Djinn, and he winks at me. "Have you found him? Have you found Dunk?"

"Is there a reward?"

"A reward? Oh, I see ... well I suppose so, yes. How does twenty-five pounds sound?"

A pause.

"It sounds low," says the man. "I was thinking more like fifty."

"Fifty!" says Mr Djinn. "That's an awful lot of money. I'm not sure I can afford fifty."

I feel sick with nerves, as if this man might somehow see me through the phone and see right through my plan. Mr Djinn sends me a look that says: *All will be well, Phyllis. All will be well.*

"That's your problem," says the man. "I'm not some free dog-finding service. If you don't want to pay, I can just let the dog go. Let him run wild and take his chances. Maybe he'll find his way home … maybe not."

This is all getting really stressful, and the thought of Dunk being set loose is a terrifying one.

Mr Djinn smiles at me calmly. *All will be fine.*

"I see," says Mr Djinn. "Well in that case, I suppose I could take some money from my savings."

"Good," says the man. "You do that. Meet me in front of the garden centre tomorrow at twelve. And make sure you've got the money with you."

"Twelve," says Mr Djinn. "How will I know who you are?"

"Bring a dog lead," says the man. "I'll find you."

And with that, he hangs up.

"The game is on," says Mr Djinn looking suddenly wide awake.

"It doesn't feel much like a game to me," I say and there is a wobble in my voice as I say it.

And now Mr Djinn says out loud what he said with his eyes just moments earlier. "All will be fine, Phyllis. All will be fine."

"So what now?" I ask.

"Now we invite the police to our little rendezvous," says Mr Djinn, lifting my phone to his ear. "Shall I call them, or will you?"

I point my finger at Mr Djinn.

"Excellent," he says. "I haven't had this much fun for about two hundred years."

Fort #52

Tomorrow we meet the man. The man will take the money. We take Dunk. And the police – if all goes to plan – take the man.

But, as I walked home from Ocean Breeze old folks' home, I thought, 'What if all doesn't go to plan?' What if all goes horribly wrong and something happens to Mr Djinn or to Dunk? And as I walked and thought and worried, a wish began to form in my mind:

'I wish I hadn't done this.'

I almost said it out loud to make it real, but something Mr Djinn said – weeks ago when he was telling his Blackbeard story – came back to me. And it was as if I could hear his voice inside my head.

'Be careful what you wish for.'

I have come to believe that Mr Djinn is very careful about what he says. He plants words like seeds, knowing they will grow and flower when the time is right. Or perhaps burying them like treasure, deep in the mind of the person he is talking to. Deep in the mind of me...

We make so many wishes every day, without even

thinking about it. Without – as Mr Djinn warns – being careful about it.

We wish for sunshine.

For a lesson to end.

For a friend to knock on our door.

For fish fingers at teatime.

We wish for lots of small things.

And I think all those small wishes are a waste of wishes.

We wish backwards too.

We wish something that has happened had not.

That we could take back something we said.

Take back something we did.

But these things are in the past and – it's a feeling I have – I don't think wishes work that way. I think wishes work forwards.

I think if you're going to wish, wish for the future.

And wish for something big.

33

The Right to Remain Silent

It's hot inside the car and we have the windows rolled halfway down. From where we are parked we can see Mr Djinn sitting in a wheelchair by a bench in front of the garden centre. Although we are trying not to stare in case we look suspicious.

Dad drums his fingers on the steering wheel. Probably because he's nervous, but the constant *pat-pat-pat* of his fingers is making me even more nervous than I already was. Which was a lot.

Mum's nervous too. "I'm worried the man won't come," she said before Dad and I left. "And I'm worried about what will happen if he does."

When I think about it like that, it's hard not to think I've done something gigantically stupid.

Pat-pat-pat go Dad's fingers on the steering wheel.

"Would you mind not doing that?" I say.

Dad looks down at his fingers as if he's surprised to find them there.

"Right, sorry."

I sigh.

Dad rubs my cheek with the backs of his fingers. "You know what you sound like when you sigh, Hedgehog?"

I shake my head. "Like someone sighing?"

"You sound like a big balloon going down." And he blows a slow and quiet raspberry. "Just like that."

"I did not do that."

"Funny, because that's what I heard." Dad kisses me in the centre of my forehead, a long firm kiss that sinks all the way to the inside of me. "Always keep your balloon full of air," he says. "It's the thing that keeps you afloat."

The clock in our car ticks on to three o'clock.

Across the car park, the police car doors open.

"Action stations," says Dad.

The police car has no police markings, so it looks like any ordinary car. And the police officers – one man and one lady – aren't wearing uniform and look just like ordinary shoppers. The lady is tiny and the man has a big belly that pushes out the front of his shirt. It's hard to imagine him chasing anybody, or her wrestling anyone to the ground. They don't look much like the police you see in movies and TV shows.

"Hopefully things won't get too … tricky," Dad says.

"Tricky?"

"You know … physical. Struggling and chasing and whatnot."

The policeman walks over to the supermarket entrance and sits on a bench not too far from Mr Djinn. The police lady stays with their car.

Dad starts *pat-pat-patting* on the steering wheel. Realizes what he's doing and stops. And then I see the man, wearing a baseball cap and sunglasses, walking slowly across the car park. I thought he would have Dunk with him, but he appears to be alone.

"Is that him?" Dad asks. "Clive?"

I nod.

The man draws level with Mr Djinn; he smiles, shakes the old man's hand and bends down so that their faces are level.

The policeman stands up from the bench and stretches.

The police lady remains by her car, but she seems very alert now.

The plan is that Mr Djinn will tell the dog-napper he couldn't get the money. This is the trap. If the man refuses to hand over the dog, the police can nab him.

But the trap won't work without a dog.

Clive straightens up. He points across the car park and we all follow the direction of his finger. Parked only a short distance from us is a dirty, bashed-up car. The back window is down just enough for someone to reach a hand through. Or for a dog to push his snout out. Which is exactly what is poking through the narrow gap. A fluffy, tea-coloured snout.

"It's Dunk!" I say. "He's in the back of the car."

"Blimey," says Dad, "this is tense."

Outside, the chunky policeman has moved to within just a few steps of Mr Djinn. He pretends he is doing something on his phone, but he is watching Clive and Mr Djinn very closely.

The police lady is leaning on her car, acting normal. But you can tell she is ready.

Clive holds out his open hand to Mr Djinn.

"He wants the money," says Dad.

Mr Djinn looks Clive in the eye and shrugs his shoulders, and I can imagine his voice as he tells Clive that he doesn't have the ransom.

Clive looks suddenly annoyed. He flaps his arms up and down, the way a child might if he's been told he has to go to bed early. He is *not* happy. He begins to walk away then suddenly changes his mind, spins around and strides back towards Mr Djinn.

"Oh no," says Dad. "This doesn't look good."

The policeman edges closer to Mr Djinn who, again, shrugs his shoulders: *sorry, no ransom.*

"He's a cool customer," says Dad.

"You can say that again," I say.

"He's a cool customer," says Dad.

But neither of us laugh. This is way too nerve-racking.

Finally, Clive throws up his arms in frustration and walks away.

The policeman says something to Mr Djinn then follows Clive across the car park.

The police lady stands up to her full height, which isn't much, and starts walking towards the bashed-up car.

Something occurs to Clive. He stops walking.

The police lady stops walking.

Clive stares at the police lady, then turns to look over his shoulder.

The policeman stops walking too.

Each looks at the other.

"Damn," says Dad. "He's seen them."

He's right. Clive turns back towards his car, walking more quickly now.

The police lady starts walking faster.

So does the policeman.

It looks like something out of a comedy film.

But still, neither of us laugh.

And then they all start running at the same time. Clive to his car, the police lady to Clive, and the fat policeman struggling along at the back. The police lady is fast. She holds something up and the light flashes off its surface.

"Her badge," Dad says.

"Stop!" shouts the police lady. "Police!"

Clive doesn't stop.

He runs straight past his car and keeps on going.

The policeman stops at the car and bends to look through the gap in the window.

The police lady continues after Clive, all the time closing the distance between them. She calls again for him to stop, but he doesn't.

And then she is right behind him.

In one smooth movement, and without slowing down, the police lady kicks out at Clive's heels. His legs wrap around each other and he goes down. Hard.

Clive rolls onto his back, clutching his knee and swearing like a pirate.

"You have the right to remain silent," Dad says,

which I assume is another police reference.

The police lady says something to the man and beckons for him to stand up, which he does, slowly. You can tell from the way he is standing that he is thinking of running again, but the police lady wags a finger at him and says something we can't hear. Clive turns around and holds his hands behind his back.

"She's going to cuff him," Dad says.

"For dog-napping?"

"For resisting arrest," says Mr Djinn's voice. He has wheeled himself across the car park and is now alongside our car.

"You were brilliant," says Dad.

Mr Djinn shrugs modestly. "I have been in tighter scrapes."

He turns his attention back to the drama.

I turn too, just in time to see the police lady fasten Clive's hands behind his back with what looks like a strip of plastic. It doesn't look like the handcuffs you see in TV programmes.

At the same time, the policeman opens the back door and Dunk comes bounding out. Fluffy, happy and not at all bothered by the drama happening around him.

I open my door to get out, but Dad says, "Just a moment, Phyll."

And I realize this drama is not over yet. The policeman is holding Dunk by his lead, but with his other hand he is reaching into the back seat of Clive's car.

"What's this?" says Dad.

From within the car, an arm emerges – a boy's arm, tanned brown apart from a white line at the wrist where he might have worn a watch or … or a seashell bracelet.

"Clark," I whisper.

"Who?" says Dad.

"Clark!" I shout, poking my head through the open window. "Clark!"

Clark turns, sees me, and freezes.

I try to read his expression, but it's not easy. Whatever he's thinking, it's nothing happy.

"Phyll?" says Clark.

"You?" says the man, turning to me.

Clark looks at me, Mr Djinn and the police. He turns back to the man, to the dog-napper, and he says the very last word I was expecting.

He says, "Dad?"

And the police lead them both away.

34

Gruffling

It's hard to sleep.

My mind keeps going over the day's drama: the nervous wait in the car, Mr Djinn, Dunk, the chase, the trip, the handcuffs, Clark.

I have so many questions. But they are mostly about Clark – whether he knew what his dad was up to, whether he is mad at me, whether I am mad at him, and whether we can ever be friends again.

It's bonkers. Over and over my mind replays the scene. And the more tired I get, the more it feels like maybe it didn't really happen. Maybe it was a bizarre dream and I am sleeping after all.

Then Dunk will snuffle, or yawn, or make a low gruffling noise.

And I realize that, yes, it really did happen.

After the chasing and arresting, Dad drove me and Mr Djinn to the police station where we each told our version of what happened to an older police officer. Mr

Djinn was extremely tired from all the day's drama, so he went first, then the police drove him home to Ocean Breeze. "I have taken rides in and upon many things," he said, as we made our goodbyes. "Big ships, small aeroplanes, several elephants and even a carpet. But never in a police car," and his tired eyes sparkled.

Dad and the policeman laughed at this, but Mr Djinn only smiled.

When it was my turn, I explained to the police about seeing Clark's dad on the beach, except, at the time, I didn't know who he was. I told them that I always saw him with a dog lead, but never a dog. I told them about the time he found Dunk in the caves, and I told how he pretended to be Dunk's owner that last time on the beach.

The police lady said I was a "regular Miss Marple", which Dad told me was a famous lady detective.

When I asked if Clark's dad would go to jail, the policeman laughed and said, no, not this time. But he would probably get a "pretty hefty" fine. Also, he said (and this was the really important part) he wouldn't be napping any more dogs.

Dad explained about Misery Guts, and the police were happy for us to take Dunk home. For maybe ten whole minutes, I thought that Dunk was ours. But in the car, driving back to our house, with Dunk in the back seat, his nose poking out of the open window and his ears flapping in the breeze, Dad told me that this was a not-forever thing. That Dunk would only be able to stay for a few days.

I asked why, and my voice came out all crying and wet.

"It's just not the right time, sweetheart."

"No," I said. "It never is."

"We'll work something out," Dad said. "In time, we'll work something out."

But I've heard that before and nothing ever changes, so I just turned away from Dad and looked out of the window.

I feel bad about that, but at the same time, I feel I was right.

At home, Mum hugged me as if I'd been away for a week not an afternoon, kissing my hair and telling me how proud she was of me and how brave I was. She made a big fuss of Dunk too and fed him some left-over meatballs that Dad had been saving for his lunch. And even though I still wanted to sulk about not being able to keep Dunk, it was hard not to laugh at the way he gobbled up the meatballs and got tomato sauce all over his whiskers.

After that, Dad tore two sides off one of our moving-house cardboard boxes, turning it into a sort of make-do dog basket. We put a picnic blanket in the bottom and took the box up to my room. Dunk went straight into it and flopped on his back, gruffling and fidgeting and wagging his tail, like this was his new home and this was a real dog basket – not a piece of torn not-forever cardboard.

"It's not fair," I say now into the darkness.

And Dunk makes a low noise in reply.

So I pull my blankets and pillow from the bed and drag them over to where Dunk's dog box is. I bundle them up so that I'm comfortable and so I can stroke Dunk from my own not-forever nest.

And then, with the dog's slow breathing close by, and his warm fur under my hand, my eyes fall closed and I sleep.

35
Feeling Awful and Feeling Worse

"It's really pretty," says Daisy.

"You're so good at this," says Margaret.

They've both joined me today in jewellery making, Daisy making a sea-glass ring and Margaret making a mess of a seashell bracelet. I don't know if this means we are friends now, but the girls formerly known as the Horribles are right – Mum's necklace does look awesome.

Of the nine pieces of sea glass, I have glued twists of wire to seven of them, turning them from polished glass pieces into proper pendants. I have one blue pendant left to make and then the centrepiece – using the red sea glass Clark gave to me on the cove.

"You could sell that if you wanted to," Margaret says.

"It's for my Mum. For her birthday."

Hilda snorts. She is sitting at the table, but she isn't making any jewellery.

"I bought my mum a *real* silver ring for *her* birthday."

I want to tell Hilda that anyone can buy a present. That it takes imagination and effort to make one. It's my instinct to tell her I don't care about what she bought her mother. But that would make me just as bad as her, so I hold my breath and count to five. And then, because I'm still angry, I count all the way to ten.

"That sounds nice," I say to Hilda.

"What would *you* know?" says Hilda.

New school is just two weeks away, and the four of us will be in the same year, if not the same class. Margaret and Daisy still play with Hilda, but something has changed between them all. Hilda used to be the leader of their group and I think Daisy and Margaret were a little scared of her, but they don't seem to be now.

"Maybe you and your boyfriend can set up a little shop together," Hilda says. She laughs and looks to Daisy and Margaret, obviously expecting them to laugh too. But they just continue working on their jewellery.

The mention of Clark – or, "my boyfriend", as Hilda puts it – makes my stomach go tight. And not in a fluttery way. I wondered if he would come to Camp Sunshine today. Maybe I even hoped he would, but I wasn't surprised when he didn't show up.

"You know his dad got arrested?" Hilda says.

And now the two girls are interested.

"What? Why?"

"Torturing dogs," Hilda says. "The whole family's weird."

"He wasn't torturing them," I say, and my voice is loud and high.

"Ooh," Hilda says. "Temper temper. No need to get huffy 'cos your *boyfriend's* dad's a maniac."

"He wasn't torturing them," I say, choosing to ignore the boyfriend bit. "He was stealing them."

"Stealing dogs?" says Daisy.

"For the reward," I say.

"Not what I heard. Not what my mum said."

The way she mentions her mother and smirks, it stirs up all the anger inside me. It brings back the day she stole my Book of Forts and laughed about my own mother. It brings back the day she tripped me over. It brings back every horrible thing she's said and every face she's pulled. I feel the anger boil inside me and fill me up until it tingles in my fingers. And I don't even try to stop it.

"Then your mum is a liar," I say.

I don't scream or shout. My voice is controlled and hard, and I like the ways it sounds.

Margaret and Daisy look at me with their mouths hanging open.

Hilda stands up from the table. "How dare you?"

"What? Am I supposed to be afraid of you?"

"You should be," says Hilda.

"You think you're special," I say. "Probably because *your mother* told you so. But you're *nothing*. No one actually *likes* you, Hilda. You're just a spoiled, spiteful and stupid girl."

Hilda's bottom lip trembles, her chin dimples and, before she turns and storms away, I see tears in her eyes.

This is the payback I wanted.

But far from feeling good about putting Hilda in her place, I feel absolutely awful.

And though I don't know it now, by the end of the day, I will feel a whole lot worse.

At lunch break, we leave our jewellery laid out where we have been working on it. But when we come back an hour later, my piece of red sea glass – my most important piece – has vanished.

Daisy and Margaret help me look for it. We go through everything on the table, root through the ice cream tubs of beads and shells and sea glass, get down on our hands and knees and search the floor. But the sea glass is nowhere.

"What you looking for?" says Hilda, but her smug smile says she knows all too well what I'm looking for.

"She's lost a piece of sea glass," Daisy says.

"Hilda," Margaret says, in the tone of voice parents use to talk to naughty children. "Do you know where it is?"

Hilda smirks. "Have you looked in the bins?"

"Why? Is that where you put it?"

Hilda shrugs. "Didn't say I put it anywhere. Just trying to be helpful, that's all."

There are four big bins in the kitchens containing different types of rubbish from recycling to food waste. Daisy and Margaret offer to help, but it's a disgusting job and it's not their fault I called Hilda all those names.

So I roll up my sleeves and I root through them all. Through torn paper, plastic bottles, mouldy bread, dirty tissues, blobs of chewing gum, dead flies, balls of fluff and heaven knows what else.

But if my piece of red sea glass is in any of the bins, I don't find it.

As we are leaving for the day, Hilda walks past me waving her hand beneath her nose. "You smell of rubbish," she says.

And you are rubbish, I don't reply.

Because hurting someone is easy. And sometimes, it might even feel good. For a moment, at least.

But it doesn't mean it's right.

"I'm sorry," I say. "For what I said."

Hilda shrugs. "Whatever."

"That sea glass is for my mum's birthday," I say. "If you've got it, can I have it back? Please."

"Why you asking me?" Hilda says. "I'm spoiled, spiteful and stupid, remember?"

And she walks away, smiling.

36
Holding Hands

In the TV shows I watch and the books I read, the bad person always loses. They get what's coming to them. And the goodie gets to have the last word and the last laugh.

Like me calling Hilda spoiled, spiteful and stupid.

But this isn't one of those stories. This is real life, and now, at the end of it all, Hilda is the one who's smiling, and I'm the one who has lost.

I called her names and she took my final piece of sea glass.

Would it have been better if I'd said nothing?

I'd still have the final piece of sea glass for Mum's necklace. Which would be good. But I wouldn't have stood up for myself. And I think that was an important thing to do.

Real life can be really confusing.

The other thing that happens in TV shows and books is that enemies become friends. They discover something in common, or one helps the other out of a tough situation, or something like that. I don't see that happening with me and Hilda. And that's fine by me.

You can't be friends with everyone. And even if you could, there wouldn't be time.

These are the thoughts swirling around my head as I leave Camp Sunshine and start walking home. I'm so deep in thought that I don't notice Clark sitting on the wall outside. Not until I've walked past him and his voice snaps me back to reality.

"You wore it," he says.

It takes me a moment, maybe half a second, to recognize his voice. And when I turn around, Clark is standing right in front of me. Smiling.

"Wore it?" I ask confused.

Clark reaches up and gently tugs at the tartan clip in my hair. "It suits you. And your hair's grown."

"Hair tends to do that," I say.

"Yeah," says Clark. "So I've heard. So … want to go to the cove?"

I have about a million questions. But where do you start with a million questions?

Clark saves me the trouble by asking one of his own.

"Are we still friends?"

"That depends," I say.

"I didn't know," Clark says. "I didn't know what Dad was up to."

I nod. "Then we're still friends." And we set off walking towards the beach.

"When did you get back?"

We are sitting on the sand, close together and looking out towards the sea. We walked here in more or less silence. Just getting used to each other again and knowing that there would be time for talking later. Knowing that it would be easier somehow with the sea in front of us.

Or maybe I was just being shy.

"We got home the day before yesterday," Clark says. "Dad came round the next morning. Him and Mum have important stuff to sort out."

"What sort of stuff?"

"Like them not ever being together kind of stuff."

"You mean..."

"They're getting a divorce."

"Why?"

Clark laughs. "Do you need to ask?"

"I suppose not."

"I love him," Clark says. "He's my dad, after all.

But he's ... well, he's trouble. Obviously."

"So why were you with him?"

"After him and Mum had finished talking – and shouting – Dad said he was going to take me for ice cream. That's the sort of thing he does, see. He goes away for ages without saying anything then comes back and thinks giving Mum a necklace and taking me for ice cream will make it okay again."

"Grown-ups are weird."

"You can say that again," Clark says. And, of course, I do, which makes Clark laugh.

"But what about Dunk?"

Clark looks out to sea.

"So we went out to Dad's car, and the dog – Dunk – he was sitting in the back seat."

"Was he okay?"

Clark nods. "Dad had left the window open a bit. He's an idiot, but he's not cruel. Anyway, he said he'd found him wandering on the beach and was going to take him back to his owner on the way to get ice cream. And, well ... you know the rest. Seeing as it was your plan after all."

"Sorry," I say. "I didn't know he was your dad. I might not have done it if I'd known."

"I'm glad you did," Clark says. "Maybe he'll sort his

life out. Although he probably won't. Mum says he's incorrigible."

"What does that mean?"

Clark shrugs. "Not sure. Stupid, I think. Anyway. I guess you got a dog out of it."

I shake my head. "We can't keep him."

"Why?"

I take a deep breath. "Not the right time. At least that's what *my* dad said."

"So what's going to happen to him?"

"He'll go to a dog's home and wait for someone to take him. Someone nice I hope."

Clark turns to me and holds out his hand. For a moment, I think he wants me to hold it, and then I remember I am still wearing his seashell bracelet. I take the bracelet off and hold it out to Clark.

He looks at it, then looks at me in confusion.

"What?" he says.

"I… I thought you wanted it back?"

Clark laughs. "No. That's yours now. I was offering to hold your hand … if that's okay?"

Blimey!

Clark is still holding his hand out to me. So I slip the bracelet back onto my wrist and place my hand in his. I've never held hands with a boy before, so I don't know if I'm even doing it right. But his hand feels nice in mine. It makes me feel a bit weird – a bit fluttery – in my tummy. But it's a nice weird. I could get used to it.

"I'm going away," Clark says.

"What? Now?"

"Next week," Clark says.

"But school starts next week. You can't go on holiday again."

"It's not a holiday." And he turns to look at me. An expression on his face that seems to say, *Sorry*. "We're moving ... to Scotland."

"Why?"

"Mum says a fresh start would be good for both of us."

A terrible thought occurs to me. "Is it because of your dad? Because of ... me? What I did?"

Clark thinks about this, he shakes his head. "It was going to happen sooner or later."

"And now it's sooner."

His hand is still in mine and I don't want to let it go. Not now and not next week.

"Maybe you can come and visit," he says.

"I'd love to."

"You can come and see my granny, she knows about a thousand rude limericks and sh—"

And he stops. He turns to me, as if something important has just occurred to him.

"What?"

"She's in an old folks' home," Clark says. "Like the one we went to that day when it was raining."

"Ocean Breeze," I say, not at all sure what Clark is getting at.

"Well, they have a dog," he says.

"Who does?"

"The old folks' home. In Scotland. All the old folks make a fuss of him and walk him and feed him biscuits. He loves it. And they love him."

"Sounds nice."

"Well, what if you could do the same for Dunk?"

I turn to look over my shoulder and, if I squint, I can just about see the shape of Ocean Breeze old folks' home perched above the cliffs. I think about how the old folk love Dunk, and how he is so happy around them.

"Do you think they'd take him?"

"Only one way to find out," says Clark. "Let's go and ask."

"Now?"

"Why not?"

Clark's hand is still in mine and I'm not quite ready to let it go. "How about in ten minutes?" I say.

Clark smiles and turns his face towards the sun. "Let's make it fifteen."

And we sit, quietly holding hands and looking out to sea.

Fort #53

I have lost Clark twice now. At least that's how it feels.

Dunk too, in a way.

Except, in his case, I have given him away: first to Clive and next to the old folks.

They said yes – of course they said yes – so in two days' time, Dunk will become the youngest resident of Ocean Breeze old folks' home.

But while Clark and Dunk are moving on, I feel as if Mum is coming back.

She read 'Treasure Island' to me tonight, making it four days in a row, and life feels almost normal. It feels almost perfect. Dunk sits in his not-forever cardboard box while Mum reads, occasionally woofing and grumbling as if he had something to say about the story. As if he was enjoying listening to Mum tell us all about the pirates and their wicked plan.

Dunk will miss the end of the story, but I will tell it to him on our walks in the cove, where the ghosts of real pirates still linger.

If I take Clark's bracelet off, I can see tiny indents in

my wrist where the shells have pressed against the skin. It's left a mark.

Like a ghost of itself, I suppose.

And I suppose, Clark has left a mark on me too. I haven't known him for ages, only a few weeks, but those few weeks have changed me — even if it's only a little bit. I'm not as confident as Clark, but I'm more confident than I used to be. And some of that is down to him.

People come and people go.

But if someone — or some dog — touches your heart, I think they change it. They leave a mark, like a ghost of themselves and of your time together.

And that never ever goes away.

Fort #54

There is something else, too, a nagging idea that my brain can't quite wrap itself around. Like an itch I can't reach. But it has something to do with wishes. That much I know for sure. And I have a feeling – a strong feeling – that it's important.

37

A New Home

"I'm so proud of you," Mum whispers into my ear.

It's the ninth time she's said it today. At least.

"If you can all squish a little closer together..." says the lady with the camera.

We are standing in the garden of Ocean Breeze, me and Mum and Mr Djinn and Dunk. And standing on either side of us, the policeman and police lady from the day we rescued Dunk. I'm holding a certificate that says: *"Awarded to Phyllis Pearson in recognition of her initiative and bravery"*.

The lady taking our picture is from the local newspaper and she's going to write about me and Dunk and the dog-napper.

"Little more," she says.

And we all squash a little tighter together. Dad had to go to work, but he said it was okay because he always looks like a criminal in photographs and people might think he was the dog-napper.

"You must be very proud," the photographer lady says to Mum.

"I am," Mum says. "Very proud."

And just as I laugh, the lady takes her picture.

"Lovely," she says. "Just lovely."

And Dunk barks in agreement.

It's a happy day, but also a sad one. This will be Dunk's first day living in Ocean Breeze. They have a proper basket for him, loads of toys and all the old folks are super happy to have him living with them. I still get to walk him whenever I want, but I can't help feeling a little sad that he won't be sleeping in my room any more.

"Such a lovely idea," the lady from the newspaper said when we told her about Dunk's new home. "Such a lovely ending to the story."

And a funny look crossed Mum's face. She looked suddenly alert, the way a dog does when it hears the word "walkies". Only the word that pricked Mum's ears up was the word "story".

After the pictures and the handshakes and the hugs and the lady from the newspaper asking questions and scribbling notes in her notebook, after all of that, the police officers and the photographer say their goodbyes and go back to catching criminals and making newspapers.

And me and Mr Djinn go inside to play cribbage. We ask Mum if she'd like to join us, but Mum says she's going to say hello to some of the old folks.

So while Mum sits and chats, and Dunk explores his new home, me and Mr Djinn play cards. He wins the first game easily, then shuffles and deals the cards for another. But I don't pick mine up just yet.

Because just like that, I have it.

My brain finally identifies and takes firm hold of the thought that was nagging like an itch last night. It's huge and exciting and crazy, and I don't know how I didn't realize sooner.

Mr Djinn looks at me and smiles. "Something is on your mind, Phyllis."

"If I ask you something," I say, "will you tell me the truth?"

Mr Djinn sits a little straighter in his chair. He says, "Ask."

"Wishes."

"Wishes?" repeats Mr Djinn.

I feel suddenly foolish, and look over my shoulder to check no one can hear what I'm about to say. Especially Mum.

"A lot's happened since ... since we became friends,"
I say. Mr Djinn smiles at this, he takes hold of my hand.
"And I wondered if you..."

He lowers his voice to a whisper. "If I have been
granting wishes?"

"Yes."

"I have told you already. I am old. My powers are
weak. Why do you ask?"

"We were looking for a book," I say. "Me and Dad
and Mum, and having so much fun, but then ... Mum
started getting sad. Like she was under a cloud."

"So you made a wish?"

"I wished the cloud would pass. And it did, right
after we found the book. It was *1001 Nights*. Just like
yours."

Mr Djinn smiles at the familiar title. "Who found
the book?"

"I picked up a box and it fell out."

"So that was you," says Mr Djinn.

"Well, sort of. Maybe."

"And why were you looking for the book in the first
place? Having all this fun?"

"Because I told Mum about you?"

Mr Djinn bows modestly. "You talked, your mother
listened, you had fun. That also was you."

"Well what about Timmy, then? The lost dog."

"What about him?"

"I wished for him to be found. And it happened."

"That is all you did? Wish?"

"Well, I phoned Nora. I told her the phone number had run on the posters."

"I recall," says Mr Djinn. "And after your most thoughtful call, Nora replaced the posters, and two days later Timmy was returned."

I nod.

"You again," says Mr Djinn.

"Are you saying wishes don't exist?"

Mr Djinn laughs and shakes his head. "I would never say such a thing. What I am saying, is that life is a story. And we each write our own, every single day. The decisions we make, the things we do and do not do. This is its own magic."

And as he says it, a shiver runs down my back.

The first time I met Mr Djinn, he told me, *"If it were easy, I would grant you three wishes in the click of a finger."*

I felt a shiver down my spine that time too. I don't know what that means, but what I do know is this:

One way or another, I have had two wishes granted since I met Mr Djinn.

Meaning, if he really is a genie – and I know he

almost definitely probably isn't – then I have one wish left. Because – as everybody knows – wishes come in threes.

Again, I look around to check Mum isn't close enough to hear me. She's chatting with the carer called Chloe, and Chloe says something that makes Mum laugh. She's been so happy lately that it makes me scared. Scared that it won't last.

So if I am to be granted one more wish, I will wish forwards and I will wish big. And I will do it now.

I turn to Mr Djinn and say, "I wish my Mum was—"

Mr Djinn squeezes my hand tighter. As if to say: *Stop*.

I stop.

"We have talked about wishes," he says. "About being careful. About how men will wish for gold, for love, for what they think they want, instead of the thing they really need. Have we not?"

"Yes."

"We have talked about love fading, money dwindling. Clouds returning."

"Yes."

"Because these wishes … money, love, even happiness … they are…" With his free hand, Mr Djinn fidgets his fingers in the air, as if he were feeling a piece of cotton or silk. "They are flimsy wishes. The best wishes" – and he looks hard into my eyes – "the best wishes are carefully made. They have weight, Phyllis. They are clear and thorough and specific. You know this word, child? Specific?"

"It means exactly."

"Exactly," says Mr Djinn. "So…" He squeezes my hand gently, as if to say, *Now, try again.*

So I close my eyes. And in my mind I form a wish:

I wish my mother could be happy more than she is sad. I wish that if the clouds come, I will know how to help them pass. And I wish they will pass quickly. I wish that we will laugh together, loud and snorty and often. To exercise her Happy and keep it strong. I wish that Mum has the energy, desire and inspiration to write every day. Because I'm pretty sure that makes her happy. I wish that, no matter how dark it gets, my mother will always remember how much we love her.

The words feel like they come from somewhere else. From somewhere beyond me, but they feel right. Although there are quite a lot of them. I hope there are not too many. I open one eye, and see Mr Djinn staring straight at me.

He smiles, nods, and the nods seems to say, *This is not too much. This has weight. This is good.*

I close my eyes again. I make the wish.

My skin tingles as if cold air has blown across it. I feel goosebumps rise on my arm. Then Mr Djinn's grip loosens on my hand.

I open one eye and look at him.

Mr Djinn winks then leans back into his chair and yawns. "Perhaps you would pass me my tartan blanket?"

"Are you cold?"

"Tired," says Mr Djinn. "A long life will do that to you."

I unfold the blanket and drape it across Mr Djinn's knees, smoothing it flat and tucking it in neatly at the edges. I pick up the thermos. "Would you like more coffee?"

Mr Djinn chuckles gently and shakes his head. "You are a good-hearted child, Phyllis. It shines through."

I never know what to say when people say nice things like this. So I say nothing. I shrug.

"A long life," he says again. "I have known many people, seen many things. And, thanks to you, I have taken a ride in a police car. Which was most enjoyable."

Mr Djinn's eyes are shining and wet. He blinks, and the smallest of tears form in the corner of each eye. Probably I should say something like "are you okay?" but I feel too embarrassed to say anything.

"I never had a child," he says. And when he blinks again, the tears clear and he smiles. "But the winds brought me you. They brought me you."

And as he says it, his eyes fall gently closed.

Dunk trots over to us, yawns, and stretches out at the old man's feet, resting his chops on Mr Djinn's slippers.

And in his sleep, the genie smiles.

38

The Feel of Sand Between Her Toes

"Blimey," Mum says, as we sit and catch our breath. "That was a *lot* of steps."

Walking home from Ocean Breeze, Mum suggested we walk down to the cove to feel the sand between our toes. But, of course, before you get to the sand you have to deal with the steps – all 461 of them.

"Sorry," I say to Mum. "I should have warned you."

"Not at all," she says. "It's beautiful. Just … beautiful."

"I think it's my favourite place," I say. "In the whole world, maybe."

We're sitting on the sand, in what might be the exact centre of the beach, looking out towards the waves. Mum puts her arm around my shoulders. What I realize, but don't say, is that today is the first time Mum has been further than the garden in our new house. And – maybe it's all the time I've spent with Mr Djinn – I sense that Mum is thinking the same thing.

She sighs, which makes me think I was right.

"You know what you sound like when you sigh?" I say.

Mum looks at me with a smile.

"Like a balloon going down." And I blow a raspberry.

Mum laughs. "Do I now?"

I nod. "You have to keep your air in," I say. "It's the thing that keeps your balloon afloat."

Mum tilts her head sideways as if trying to get a better look at me. "Where did that come from?"

"Dad," I say.

Mum nods at this and is quiet for a moment. Then she nods again, as if answering a question she has just put to herself. "Where would we be without him?" Mum says.

I don't know if I'm meant to answer this and, if I am, I don't know how. So I don't try, I just sit beside Mum watching the waves. Mum scoops up a handful of sand and watches as it slides between her fingers.

"I'm sorry we didn't keep Dunk," she says. "It's been … hard."

"I know. And it's okay."

"Really?"

"He's happy," I say. "The old people love him."

"They really do," Mum says.

"And I can still walk him. So … it's okay. It's good."

Mum kisses the top of my head. "You're a special girl, Hedgehog."

She hasn't called me that for so long. And it feels like … like she's come back from somewhere. Like she's returned to me. I look at her face as she looks out to sea, she squints against the sun, but her mouth is set in a small and easy smile.

And then the smile changes into something else, like she has something she wants to say.

"What is it?" I ask.

"I have some news of my own," Mum says. "I spoke to Chloe today. At Ocean Breeze."

"I saw."

"Well, I'm going to do some work there."

"That's … that's amazing, Mum."

"Just a day or two, at first," she says. "I like it there, and it'll be good for me to … to have something to focus on."

"What about writing?"

Mum digs her hands in the sand, and she's made a pretty deep trench now. "Writing is always there. But it can be … I don't know. Lonely, maybe. It'll be nice being around people, while Dad's at work and you're at school. Nice to do something for someone else. And anyway," she says, and her smile spreads. "They have such wonderful stories. So maybe they'll do something for me. Inspire me, perhaps."

"You should talk to Mr Djinn," I say. "His stories are the *best*."

"He seems an interesting soul."

When I first told Mum and Dad about Mr Djinn, I never told them that he claimed to be a genie. I'd worried that they might think he was crazy and stop me going to visit. I worried that they'd laugh at me, or him. But now, I don't know what it is, but I'm not worried about that any more.

"He says he's thousands of years old," I say.

Mum laughs, but not a teasing laugh. Just a short gentle sound. "Thousands?"

"He says he's a genie."

"As in a three wishes, magic lamp, Aladdin kind of genie?"

"Uh huh. Says he knew Blackbeard the pirate, had twelve wives and owned a tiger. All sorts."

"He sounds very interesting," Mum says, and her expression flickers again, the way it did when the photographer said the word "story".

"Maybe later, you can tell me some more about this Blackbeard business."

"Really?"

"Really," Mum says. "*The Genie and the Pirate*. It might make an interesting story, don't you think?"

A breeze blows in, stirring the sand and sending two gulls circling upwards into the sky. Despite the sun, the breeze is cold as ice and it makes me shiver from the bottom of my back to the roots of my hair.

"It's gone cold," says Mum, scooping up another fistful of sand. "Ouch. What's...?"

She opens her hand to reveal a piece of the most beautiful sea glass. Almost black, but a deep dark blue when she holds it up to the sun. It's shaped like a teardrop – fat at one end, pointed at the other – and covered in a criss-cross pattern of raised lines.

"Sea glass," I say.

Mum hands it to me. "The edges are perfectly smooth," she says. "Feel."

"This one must be very old," I say. "Can I have it?"

"It's yours," Mum says.

But two days from now, I will give it back to her. As the centrepiece of her birthday necklace. It's perfect – as if this is the piece I've been waiting for all along.

39

A Very Long Sleep

I miss Dunk already, so I walk down to the old folks' home straight after breakfast the next morning. But even before I open the door, something feels different. As if the building itself has gone quiet. Not just the sounds from within, but the bricks and windows, the door and the gardens outside. As if everything has been washed in sadness.

And I know. Before I see anyone with a sad and sorry face, before I see Mr Djinn's empty armchair, I know. I have an urge to turn and walk away. To hurry home. To run all the way. But I push the door open and step inside.

In the reception area, I press a buzzer and wait, a sickly feeling in my tummy.

I don't know how long it takes for someone to come, but I'm relieved to see it's Chloe. Of all the carers, she's the friendliest. And I think she liked Mr Djinn the most.

When she comes through the door, her face is

turned down and her shoulders are drooped. She says nothing, but opens her arms to me and when I go to her, she hugs me and I smell tea and biscuits and warm blankets on her apron. She hugs me tight, and even though I can't see her, I can feel her crying – the soft in-out of her belly and the gentle sound of her sniffing back tears.

"I'm sorry," Chloe says. "I'm so sorry."

She squeezes me one last time, then lets go of the hug and uses her apron to wipe the tears from my cheeks. I didn't even know I was crying until she did this, and now that I know, I cry even harder, the tears rolling down my cheeks and dripping onto my T-shirt.

"When?" I ask.

"Yesterday," she says. "Not long after you left."

"How?"

"In his sleep," Chloe says. "He died in his sleep."

And now that the word has been said, I feel as if I have been slapped. A mixture of shock and pain and anger is how it feels, and all I want to do is lie on the floor and curl up into a ball. Chloe is squeezing me by the upper arms and it feels like she is the only thing holding me up.

"In his favourite chair, with his blanket on his knees, Phyllis. Dunk curled up at his feet, the sun bright in the sky outside. I think he was ready, Phyllis. And I think it was quite lovely. Quite a beautiful way to go."

And then Dunk appears. He trots through the doorway to the main hall, his steps slow and his head hung low. Like he knows too. He huffs out a small noise that's not exactly a bark. More like a sad, quiet hello.

"Hey, Dunk," I say. "Are you ready for your walk?"

Dunk lifts his head to look at me. And now he barks, all sadness forgotten. Everything is about the walk now. It's all that exists. He barks and turns in a circle, his tail wagging like a flag in the wind.

Fort #55

Mr Djinn said he had not granted any wishes for me. And I suppose I know that this is true. That he wasn't a genie at all – just a kind and wise old man who was very good at reading faces and telling stories.

But maybe that is a kind of magic, after all.

He said, too, that genies can't grant wishes for themselves but I wonder, if they could, what would he have wished for himself this summer?

I think I know the answer.

The first time I met him, Mr Djinn said this summer would be his last.

That he had lived a long and full life, and that now he was tired. Now he was ready.

"Being a genie is tiring work," he had said. "And soon I will sleep for ever."

That was the happy ending he wanted for himself. Maybe he even wished for it.

While I was sitting on the beach with Mum, while she dug her fingers through the sand and found the fragment of sea glass that will finish her necklace, Mr Djinn slept.

Perhaps he dreamed — of tigers, and pirates and the fat wives that went before him. I hope he did. I hope he was dreaming when he breathed his last breath.

Perhaps I should be happy for him.

But if I could have one more wish, I would wish to see Mr Djinn one last time.

So I could tell him thank you.

For being my friend.

For helping me when I was lost.

For showing me that life is a story.

And that we can write our own happy endings, if we believe enough in ourselves.

I wish I could see Mr Djinn one last time so I could tell him all of this.

And so I could tell him that I loved him.

40

Surprises

Mum's birthday is on a Saturday, which, if you ask me, is the best day of the week for this kind of thing. We have a late breakfast all together in the garden – croissants with jam and peanut butter – and the sun is already high and warm when Mum opens her presents.

She cries when I give her the necklace, big, happy tears that catch the sun and roll down her cheeks. She holds the necklace up to the light and the glass casts stripes of colour across her face.

"This one," Mum says, holding the deep blue teardrop that she found herself just two days ago.

"I know," I tell her. "I think it was waiting for us to find it."

Mum laughs and cries at the same time and the noise is a sloppy wet snort that makes us all laugh.

"You're beautiful when you snort," Dad says, and he gives her a big kiss which goes on long enough to be quite embarrassing.

"And this," I say, sliding a small wrapped present towards Mum.

She pretends to weigh it in her hands, then holds it to her ear and shakes it, even though it's pretty obviously a book.

Mum has read to me every night for a week now, and yesterday she spent three hours in her study with the door closed. Which is a good sign. Mum only closes her study door when she's writing. When she came out, she was smiling. "Four pages," she said, holding up the same number of fingers.

"Are they good pages?" I asked.

Mum waggled her hand up and down. "I'm a bit rusty," she said. "But … yeah, I think they're pretty good."

I didn't ask if she was writing about Mr Djinn because the question would make me cry. And anyway, I just know that she is.

I miss him terribly. His silly stories about being a genie, which, now that he's gone, I suppose were just that. Stories. But he gave them to me, and now I've given them to Mum.

They will bring her happiness. Just like I wished for when I last saw Mr Djinn.

When I think about him – his brown skin and

warm eyes, his deep and friendly voice – I feel my mouth fill with sadness and sometimes I cry. I have dreamed about him too, and in the dream he is young and strong and surrounded by smoke. In my dreams, he is the genie he always claimed to be.

Last night, wrapping presents, I asked Dad if Mum was better now. And his answer surprised me.

"It's not that simple, Hedgehog."

Dad told me that Mum was doing well, but that the clouds can always come back. And they probably will. "But they will be further apart," he said. "And, if we're lucky, they will clear more quickly."

So long as we're there for her, Dad said, the clouds will always clear.

"Because we keep each other afloat," I said.

"That's right, Hedgehog. That's exactly right."

Mum tears open her present now and slides the notebook out from inside the paper. There is a hot air balloon on the front, shaped like an upside-down teardrop and striped in yellow and green and red.

To keep you afloat, I think.

Above the balloon, I stuck a white sticky label, and on this, in my best capitals, I have written FORTS.

"Forts?"

"Like thoughts," I say. "And like, well, forts as well."

And I tell Mum what Hevver the counsellor told me about a hundred years ago – or at least that's how it feels – that writing your thoughts down can make them easier to understand. And I tell her my idea about thoughts being like forts – something strong, something to keep you safe.

"That's beautiful," Mum says. "Really beautiful." And she kisses me and pulls my head close to her chest where it's soft and warm and perfect.

When Mum lets me go, Dad asks if she can handle one more present. And Mum says she thinks she can manage.

Dad tells us to follow him, and when we get up from the table in the garden, he leads us inside, to the closed door leading into the room where all those weeks ago we searched for a battered old copy of *1001 Nights*.

Where, if you believe in that kind of thing, my first wish came true.

"Ready?" says Dad.

And before we can tell him that we are, he opens the door. He opens the door onto a room I have never seen. Or at least not like this.

The room has been painted blue – a calm, greeny-blue that makes me think of the ocean. There are blinds on the windows, but they are rolled up, letting in the floods of morning sunshine. And the walls ... the walls are lined with shelves that weren't there a few weeks ago. The shelves are lined with books. Books that were lying in piles and heaps and sitting in boxes.

"A library room," Mum says.

"I stacked them in alphabetical order," Dad says. "By title. But, we can change it if—"

"It's perfect," Mum says. "It's ... perfect."

She's crying again, but she's smiling too, and when she kisses Dad this time, it goes on so long I have to look away.

When we call Gran and Granddad after supper, we call from what is now officially known as the library. We don't have armchairs yet, or a sofa, so we sit on blankets on the floor and turn the computer around so Gran and Granddad can see the shelves that Dad made and fixed to the walls entirely in secret. Gran says maybe Dad can come and put some shelves up for her, because Granddad will never get round to it, which makes all the grown-ups laugh.

"Anyway," says Gran, drawing the word out extra-long so it sounds like *aaaanywaaaay*. "We have something to show you."

The screen goes all crackly as Gran gets up with her computer and then we are following her through a door, down a corridor and into another room.

The camera is pointing away from Gran and Granddad but we can still hear their voices. "What can you see, Phyll?" Gran says.

"Nothing yet," I tell her.

As I squint at the screen, I realize Mum and Dad are looking at me, not the computer. As if they already know what this is about.

A thought forms in my mind.

"Is it...?"

And then the picture comes closer and I see it. I see *them*.

Josie the farm dog lying in a basket and, at her tummy, three or maybe four small shapes like gently wriggling sausages.

"Puppies?" I say. And the word, when it comes out of my mouth, is so small and so quiet that I have to say it again. "Puppies!"

"Five of 'em," says Granddad. "And not a week old between them."

I see them clearly now – *five* perfect puppies, all folded in against each other and squashed up against their mummy's tummy.

"Maybe we'll bring one when we come to visit," Gran says, and I laugh.

But no one else laughs.

"What about this one?" Gran's hand reaches into the picture and gently lifts one of the puppies. The picture goes all weird again for a second, then it's facing Gran and Granddad, only now, Gran is holding the puppy. It fits easily in one of her hands, its eyes are closed and it is, easily and by a very long way, the cutest, most adorable thing I have ever seen in my life.

"He's…" There's only one word for it. "He's adorable. Wait, is he a boy?"

"He is," says Mum. "And he's yours."

"What? Wait? I…"

"November," Dad says. "Gran and Granddad are coming to visit in November."

"No one told me," says Granddad.

"You paid for the tickets," says Gran. "You great fool."

"Did I?" says Granddad. "That was nice of me. December, you say?"

"November," says Gran, shaking her head.

"My birthday's in November," I say.

"That's right, Hedgehog."

"Is this a joke?"

Dad shakes his head, Mum too. "It's not a joke. More of a … a birthday present."

"For me?"

He nods. "For you."

I can't believe it, I'm crying all over again, and if this carries on much longer I'll cry myself dry.

"In just over three months," Mum says, "you'll have another dog to walk."

"And clean up after," says Dad.

"Should be just about long enough to think up a good name," says Mum.

But I already know his name. "He's called Mr Djinn," I say.

"Of course he is," says Mum.

41

Treasure

When I go to collect Dunk for his walk, I feel the sadness of losing Mr Djinn all over again. But it's a little less this time. A tiny bit less, and maybe the next time I come, it will be less still.

I clip on Dunk's lead and we're just about to walk out of the home when Chloe comes running after me.

"I almost forgot," she says. "He … this was in his room." She hands me a small brown-paper parcel tied in string. On the top is a small cardboard tag, and handwritten on the tag is my name.

"You're the only Phyllis that comes here," Chloe says. "So it must be you."

Dunk tugs at his lead, not at all impressed by this delay to his walk.

"Okay, boy. I understand."

I put the parcel in my backpack and lead Dunk through the sliding doors and out into the warm evening.

The parcel is never far from my thoughts, but I try to push it to the back of my mind. Not that I don't want to open it, not that I'm not *desperate* to know what's inside, more that I don't want to know *yet*. Perhaps because when I open it, when I see what it is Mr Djinn left to me, then that part of my life – that story – comes to an end.

So I wait.

While Dunk runs and splashes in the sea, I run with him, my bag bouncing lightly on my back, the parcel inside just out of reach, just out of sight of my mind's eye.

Tonight after I came back from walking Dunk, I hung my bag on a peg in the hallway and said nothing about it to Mum or Dad, otherwise they might have encouraged me to open it. And I had the sense by then that this was something I should open alone.

We ate supper in the garden and the low sun sparkled through the nine glass pendants on Mum's necklace – pale blue, green and white. And the larger, teardrop-shaped piece shining with a deeper blue that brought to mind the sea at night.

At bedtime, Mum read the final chapter of *Treasure Island*, she tucked me into bed, stroked my eyelashes closed and whispered, "Sleep well, Hedgehog. And watch out for pirates."

But, of course, I can't sleep.

The sun sets over the sea here and as it does, the stars on my curtains fade from white to black to nothing at all. Only then do I slip quietly out of bed. Mum and Dad are in the library – I can hear low music and soft voices – so I take the stairs slowly, silently. Like Jim Hawkins from *Treasure Island*, perhaps, sneaking about in the dark, looking for treasure and avoiding pirates.

I find my bag where I left it, hanging on a hook just inside the front door, and I carefully unzip it and remove the small, brown-paper package. No pirates stir. No one calls the alarm, and I go slowly up the stairs and close the door to my room.

I open the curtains just wide enough to let in a thin slice of moonlight. The moon is half hidden tonight, hanging over the sea like a watchful eye. But it's bright enough that I can read my name on the cardboard tag.

I pull the string and slip the bow. The paper rustles as I unwrap it to reveal a small wooden box – just big enough to hold a bracelet, a hair grip or a funny rubber. But somehow I know that it contains none of these things. It has a sliding lid on the top and whatever's inside is packed in cotton wool, which I remove next.

And now, from the wooden box, I carefully lift a small glass bottle.

It looks black in the dim light, with a raised criss-cross pattern on the surface. The bottle is sealed with a cork, but when I pull this, it remains tight in place. As if it has been there for a very long time, so long that it has forgotten how to come loose. Around the neck of the bottle is a metal ring that might once have been attached to a chain.

A memory swirls up from the bottom of my mind. Like sand, if you like, from the ocean bed. I remember Mr Djinn's tale of Blackbeard. Of how the pirate asked no wishes, but kept his genie – kept Mr Djinn – corked inside a bottle that he wore on a chain around his neck.

Outside, a strong gale whistles through the trees and rattles the glass panes in my window. The sea is hidden from view, it lies 1000 steps away, maybe even 1001, just out of sight beyond the green fields and old bent trees that look like pirate ships in the night. I can't see it, but I know it's there.

And if I listen carefully, I can hear the waves behind the wind.

I remember how Mr Djinn said the bottle one day slipped from Blackbeard's neck, and tumbled into the ocean where a sea storm tossed it against the rocks

("Like a pea in a pot") knocking a hole clean through the side.

And Mr Djinn – if you believe the story, if you believe a man can be a genie – was free.

Beyond my window, the trees sway and bend and bow.

When I last saw him, Mr Djinn said, "The winds brought me you."

But that's not exactly right. I think the winds, and the tides, brought him to me.

I turn the bottle over in my hand, feeling its gentle weight and heavy history. There is a hole in the side; perfectly smooth and shaped like a teardrop.

Holding the bottle so that it catches the moonlight, I see – of course – that glass is not black, but a dark, deep blue.

Like the sea at night-time.

Fort #56

I believe.

Andy Jones is the author of five novels for adults, and he hopes you will read them all when you're grown-up. This is his first novel for children (so far). He is also the author of *Unleash Your Creative Monster* – a children's guide to writing. Find out more at www.andyjones.com

On Twitter:
@andyjonesauthor
@WalkersBooksUK